The Yellow Verandah

The Yellow Verandah

A novel by Donya Lyttle

Santa Barbara / 1986

Printed in the United States of America.

Library of Congress Cataloguing in Publication Data
Donya Lyttle, 1927 -
THE YELLOW VERANDAH
I. Title.
PS3562.Y47Y4 1986 813'.54 86-14318
ISBN 0-936784-16-4
(paperback) ISBN 0-936784-17-2

Published by FITHIAN PRESS
A division of John Daniel, Publisher
Post Office Box 21922
Santa Barbara, CA 93121

To H.S.
for the initial encouragement
and to J.W.
without whose abiding interest the book
would not have been written.

"Why not dream a little?"
—Jean

from Jean's Journal

December 1. And, now the problem of living. How should we live? Do we have to live alone? Do people always leave?

Dec. 29. Well...I'll start with verbs, 'love' and then 'hate.' Certainly I don't hate. And I'll stick with learning more of the 'cosmos' for the order of my universe.

Jan. 1. I should drift back to the first group, but I'm turned off by the immensity of the problems. There was that one woman who broke out in tears over the fact that her husband had taken her two children away from her. The group had sprung up as a haven from a society which excluded them. But how could I help? I am unable to extend myself to harboring three people, or girls who had no place to stay. I'd exhaust myself. I can't make a 'clubhouse' out of my home.

Jan. 6. I wish I could change somehow, get out and create a new community, where we could enjoy each day and get some beauty in our lives....

Feb. 9 Now what are you mooning about for, depressing yourself? You've learned long ago that this time alone was meant to be for personal creativity, that this was the only time you ever produced anything. Better yet, why not devise a plan that would make things more livable for a lot of people. You're just feeling sorry for yourself. Get out there and go to work. But the oldness, the oldness! Jean, what you need is a counterpart, one with some charisma to get things moving....

Feb. 12. "And, I feel a sense of relief
Talking about all this, but
I haven't really told you how my knees
Do ache in this rain, oh
Not a lot, and the pain isn't unbearable."

Feb. 13. I remember this weekend as we headed back home, rain clouds at our car windows, listening to the radio, how colder parts of the country were reported at minus 85 degrees. But as we came back into the desert, a smoky pall fell into dusk and early night. Our heads were full of promising plans, and we forgot we were supposed to be depressed by the weather. Our plan was shaping up, this having a centralized place for people in music and for all women's music, so tantalizing. Just an idea, but my dream lay in chrysalis in the cocoon of Llangolen West on the California coast.

March 1. Here is the idea. Now the energy Drew can bring to the plan; this is needed to make Llangolen West a reality.

March 13. If I could imagine a three-room writing space, allowing a broad desk out on the verandah where I could contemplate a long sweep to the sea...ah...that would be contentment, some place in the middle of a big field. Alongside the typing desk would be a flat space to spread things out. I see a stand with just one blue vase holding a hydrangea. Then in the back would be a large living-eating-entertaining room. I could discipline and organize my thinking on that yellow verandah!

—Jean

Prologue

Wonder what my next major move is, Drew thought to herself, not out loud to her companion, one and a half feet shorter. What could be my next adventure? I've spent the first years in the L.A. basin. I've taken in types of humanity into my home, compulsive drinkers, clinging vines, a domineering school teacher. What is ahead?

Drew confided little of her anxiety to her partner. She kept her moods hidden, preferring to announce after she had decided what they were going to do next.

I know I'm fated to do something radical, she pursued the thought determinedly. I'm sick of that desert town. Ready for change. In fact, there is everything lacking. I'm astonished to think nine years have slipped by, and I haven't fulfilled a promise to myself.

Tall, about five feet eleven, Drew had tawny gold hair with short curls which feathered to her ears. Her long back showed a suppleness and athletic power. In earlier times she would have been termed an Amazon.

She was approaching a seaside road that led to a great rock. Her companion pressed hard to keep up the pace. As Drew approached the road curve, the Pacific waters merging from deep royal blue turned into a shimmering emerald, and farther out a glowing aquamarine strip ended the spot where sea turned into sky. Her mind was adrift with an old family legend. It went like this: An aunt, Cassandralike, had foretold that this curly-headed blonde baby would do something astonishing in her life, something to amaze the world. The tale continued by saying that she would be surrounded by water instead of desert, and that she would lose her life on a rock much as the Sappho legend on a Greek island.

To go on, Drew recalled that the aunt was rich; she had made a large fortune in real estate, and she was considered odd because she dressed rather too youthfully for her age. She jangled with gold jewelry. Part of her eccentricity had to do with a reputation of seeing into the future. When this prophetess beheld the baby, Drew, she foretold a strange future for her. Then the aunt had died.

Now, as Drew was walking along the edge of Morro Rock, some wisps of this legend floated into her mind. There was something about a rock, she thought, and she remembered there was foretold that an accident would take place. But she would recover, and then it was predicted she would carve out some different art form that would be of great interest to her confreres who had the same interests as she did.

Drew scuffed at the dirt of the road and as she continued around a cement breakwater embankment at the base of the Morro, she recalled that there was something more. The aunt had also predicted a dragon-like creature which harassed a community would have to be put away by the girl when she grew up. The dragoness would regard her as a carcass to put into her personal psychological stew.

This niece, in continuing the prophesy, would be able to thwart and destroy the repulsive creature, purely by her cleverness, thus ridding the country-side of a troublesome menace. The dragon would thereupon ruinously destroy her own health, leaving Drew to pursue her life's work.

This story, which had been repeated while Drew was still a little girl, had yet another part, one that the family had pondered in secret. It was of something to be murmured about late at night over the dinner table, hinted at. There was something unfeminine about the youngest member of the family. They never spoke of it around outsiders, but pretended that what they saw could not be seen by others.

In the meanwhile, Drew had pursued a searching existence which led through the larger city of L.A. and had brought her here to this rock with Dee Dee. Now the story loomed up like this rock. It had faded because the family hushed up the story. As Drew came into adolescence, she grew lanky, almost boy-like. The story was treated as a joke; then it faded away entirely. Drew faintly remembered something about an unconventional marriage, something to shock.

The story flickered, then was gone again as Drew and her companion, Dee Dee, began a climb that led away from the sea.

CHAPTER ONE

Breaking Off

Three hours away from Drew, a friend named Jean was in a quandary of her own making. She was busily trying to understand the harsh break-off of a friendship which had occupied all of her time in the fall. Now she was left alone again.

I've been in this place before, she groaned. I've felt like this. Only before, the pain was much, much worse. I was so numb then I had to be carried around and helped into my clothes, shown how to buy groceries for myself so that I could feed myself, helped into a strange apartment, and forced to see the psychiatrist for a few sessions.

Now I understand, she lectured herself, after that night when the wined talk came out in a gush, Kate was really taking a 90-degree turn-around away from me. Lying on a bed in her own apartment, she wished she could talk to Drew about it, but she couldn't find her. My question is: why such a build-up? Why so many phone calls, and why had she filled all my hours so that I had no room for any other friendship?

She remembered that they had gone to every show in town, even taking an hour that wasn't programmed into something else, went to the library where a new Sackville-West *Letters to Virginia* was discovered. Jean flopped back down. Drat. Where did Drew get off to? Got someone new, I expect.

She dialed Drew's number and got no response. Why such a build-up, then the arm-folded silence after a certain admission the night before? Jean reached for her notebook. Of course you could see it, but you didn't care, because she was lots of fun. You threw everybody else over and they weren't going to keep calling.

What a fool I've been, not seeing a blow coming, worse than a hundred small ones; it couldn't make up for the kindnesses before. How long had Kate planned that coup de grâce? Maybe that aura of ignoring Christmas was a warning. Those folded arms told it all. Jean paced from bedroom to kitchen.

Just deduce that this is a ploy perfected in the early seventies.

The technique is: you are to give your quarry a chase every day by calling at the same time; then all of a sudden you don't call. Next, leave the other one wondering what she did wrong. Stupid, kid-like trick, but I'm so old-fashioned and stupid, even after knowing some hard customers.

Meanwhile, through the first days of agony and then of acceptance, Jean took up the skeins of her solitary life, pouring things that hurt into her diary or her journal, and the familiar set of pen to paper did its work. The moods of others were then somehow understandable and their cruelty now more bearable.

I just need my own plan, a gyroscope to stabilize my spin. She puttered around the house the fifth day of vacation. I have to get back to work again and emotionally accept the fact that I do have friends, a small cave room of my own on the coast, the midwestern lake cottage which needs the frontage developed. I've had experience with small infidelities before.

Still, she wasn't quite through with all this yet. Never have I had so much negotiation about mutual lives, planning vacations together, correction in dress or diet, exercise guide for staying slim. Aha! She was projecting her own insecurities onto my person. Finally she ended with the psychological term "closure." She had used that; it seemed so final. Now that it was over, it brought relief.

Jean stewed and muttered, hurt, getting rid of the pain, exorcising, savoring injustice....What about the time at the liquor store when we were looking for sherry, and then we found those porn magazines, all those boys and girls together in mixed poses. We giggled over those for an hour, the shopkeeper behind us noticeably opening his boxes. We ignored him; all of a sudden we were whooping with sexual stimulation. What about that? This is where the hurt came. She had held back that kind of experience, not discussing things such as that with me, not including me.

She was going back still further, years back. Then why all the enticement. I did feel something. I think she brushed her breasts by me deliberately, a calculation, a real seduction.

This is where I got lured. I was being used, and I didn't know it, to the full, until she sat there at breakfast with her arms crossed.

She was about at the end of it now.

That's what was telling me I was worthless, unappreciated. I decided, or was it decided for me, that I had better not go to Europe with them. It took some loving people to prop me up, to bring me to the realization of my full powers.

Darn, Jean, you've allowed that before. You need a better excuse for yourself this time. She moved to her writing desk. And you don't have to feel so old. You can do it; you know how to write. The open page of Greek lay before her as a self-imposed task. This was a stupefyingly hard language to learn, but she and another were learning it together.

Well . . . I'll start with verbs, 'love' and then 'hate.' Certainly I don't hate. And I'll stick with 'cosmos' for the order of my life and my universe.

CHAPTER TWO

A City Weekend

I can't do this alone though. Now where did Drew go? Doesn't answer her phone. Jean was exasperated. Something was needed to bridge this trauma. A diversion was called for.

Finally Drew called. "Do you want to go to San Francisco?" She suggested four days of cavorting around the hilled city with Miles, her friend.

They were unexpectedly late, as Drew had to get her "eyes in," which was a euphemism for straightening out her person after tumbling around in bed; she had a new conquest and was slowed down that morning.

Jean came to Drew's house and observed her. She had an assertive face and a non-impulsive manner as she packed the few shirts and jeans into a blue nylon air-travel bag. This, together with backpack, were her few requirements.

Within five hours they had traveled out of the valley fog into the Livermore Valley; soon they were crossing the Bay Bridge. Effortlessly they entered the traffic down town, crossing Market Street. Soon they turned into the Bush Street parking lot near Chinatown.

Upstairs their friend Miles, splendidly mustached and with crisp sideburns, heated up a casserole and a downstairs pizza, while they finished the night watching Leontyne Price singing her final performance of her career, the Aida. She was sixty and retiring with that aria. Miles, sneering and chortling at her thick lips, never respectful, "the better to kiss your vulva, dear."

Leontyne Price waited professionally at the aria's end, waiting for the swelling applause, not breaking down, but some tears glistening.

The three of them spent the next day in Macy's, getting a fix of shopping. Miles was deft and assertive in the shoe department. Within six minutes, no more than ten, a two-inch pump, blue, with no trim, was chosen for Jean. Tasteful, there was no question. From there they proceeded to lingerie, Miles not so helpful now, but restive as Drew took her time on two sets of ribbed 1930 men's underwear.

"Are you bored or will you come with us to Castro Street?" Drew got Miles to agree.

They discussed for twenty minutes how to get Miles' ponderous Lincoln to a garage to pick up the second car because of the parking problem. Jean noted that some things about a small town are infinitely desirable. It's better not to have a car here.

At noon they jounced three abreast along the Castro intersection to an oyster bar. Most of the men on the crowded street had the same mustache style as Miles; most had on identical leather jackets and Levis. Miles waved and talked to six men as they walked by. This was his familiar neighborhood.

During this one day's encounter, Jean felt her self-confidence slipping. A sense of being an underling began to pervade her as Miles' sophistication forced itself down on her. She knew they admired her capabilities down underneath, but as the weekend progressed, the talk of the European trip they might share together receded as it became apparent they didn't want her along.

By the evening of the second day, this was resolved when she said, "Maybe it'd be better if the two of you went together."

Drew filled right in after with, "Well, you'll have to be quicker. With Miles, it's 'snap, snap.' "

Toward evening they picked up groceries in Castro Street and took them to the Edwardian house that belonged to Miles' lover. At a great mahogany table he presented dishes, covered porcelain filled with gravy, mashed potatoes, broasted chicken, zucchini squash. Later, over rich fresh coffee they munched homemade Lebkuken and fudge. In the massive bay window they had set up a flocked tree; below it was set up an heirloom 1900 train track with complete old-fashioned train.

After three hours of conversation, the entire effect began to sink in upon Jean, as the conversation swirled around the subject of Oakland, the running of the city. Miles had been taken aside by his boss who explained the necessities of his job, how he was to let no scandal rear up, even though they knew that he lived in San Francisco. He should be a sensible, prudent member of his community while he had such a responsible position as keeper of records. To keep his job viable, he should not do anything to disturb the mayor's office.

This evening was quiet, the tempo of a hundred years ago. No bar-hopping or looking for excitement this time.

The next day a pervasive feeling of being left out, alone, never to have a real companion, crept over Jean as she managed the car down the endless Highway Five, covering the entire valley. Some showers of rain spattered the windshield. During the drive an alleviating discussion of how unresolved things stay to discolor our future relationships helped their long journey, but the separate feeling that Drew was fantasizing about her very recent conquest, Eiko, remained in Jean's mind.

That force of sexual demand tinges everything else. She knew that although Drew was by her side, her thoughts had to be dwelling on new underwear clashes with her new friend, Eiko.

Jean reminded herself inwardly, people who need to lower others to raise their own esteem are not right to be around for any period of time. Forget them, because their emptiness will destroy you. Half the world can be so negative. I have to protect my flank against them, stave off the down people. Even so, the downpour on the car roof lowered her spirits.

Sad. But alone only for a day, a toot of a car in the drive outside began an upward turn for her as Mary Jo, where Jean hadn't spent the holidays, dragged in boxes of belated Christmas cheer. The endless giving of presents had not been avoided after all. Soon a book, the latest on Hemingway, was brought out in return, and a threatened friendship was mended. Jean's mood lightened.

But that feeling of loneness, no future, no tie to anyone, lingered. A deep gloom settled over her. Extreme loneliness!

Maybe if I'd eat it might help. She laid out a soft roll from the oven and arranged some freshly roasted beef.

Then a surprise happened, a miracle; the telephone rang. What a surprise. Someone perhaps lonelier than she, from two time zones away, in New Orleans, gave a satisfying call. She only thought she had been separated from this mind. A human voice; they talked it out. The aloneness was dissipated for a short time. It now was definitely gone.

There it was. The existential dilemma, alone in a strange place in a town that was a black town for a white person. New Orleans. The fear of what was in the streets. How many risks to take?

At one point in the conversation the connection was strained and almost broken as Jean voiced her need.

"If I come visit, I can't sleep on the floor, not at my age..."

Long pause. "Not at my age," she repeated.

Kate answered after a horrible pause... "Listen to me. I will get a futon mattress when I furnish this place in the Quarter. By Mardi Gras. Don't worry about it." Kate was taken aback, but could cope with Jean's assertions. Jean had pushed when she needed; it made it better to state out front what she had to have. It worked. Kate didn't hang up on her. The conversation was allowed to continue, comforting them both. At least, they were both very good friends, both thinking about the other. Kate expressed a need for mail, some connecting lifeline.

Hmm... Jean reflected. There was some admission of weakness. Things were going to be all right after all. They both looked forward to a reunion in a month; there was going to be a third person going.

Because of this call there was a lifeline now. There was a link out of the emptiness. Increasing her fulfillment of life-giving force, she was looking forward to Mardi Gras. At the end Kate made an allusion to that perfect gift book, the affair that had been between Virginia and Vita, the very slightest admission that such relationships did occur and had happened between very famous people. Maybe you could call it a romantic friendship. People needed families other than fathers and mothers. Kate told Jean to leave her—Kate's personal belongings—in Jean's extra bedroom; there was some sense of returning. The question of what was ahead of both of them was still unanswered, but there was hope now.

Jean helped Kate's sense of estrangement by giving her direct advice that it might take weeks and months before it meant anything, this leave, what it was all about, and Jean acknowledged that yes, one always looked around for a familiar face. When her arranged schooling started, the agony of separateness would subside.

An arrangement was made for Jean to make the next call, directly into the brick-walled womb that was Kate's new apartment for the next six months. The phone connection was clicked off, but the human connection was on.

Jean settled things with herself in that . . . I guess I am fated not to have an important other, no counterpart exists.

CHAPTER THREE

A Contracting Consciousness

Into February after her return from San Francisco, Jean was still outside any group. You don't know how these others feel. They are all in a race with each other, she told herself.

Drew had a new liaison, a woman named Eiko, having met her at a big party, and had seemingly shut out Jean altogether. The new lover, Colombian-Japanese, had been in America for twenty years and had been a Bay Area woman, living in the hills above Berkeley. She was pretty, with masses of black hair which was beginning to gray.

Jean looked at the situation, decided the intensity of the relationship precluded many old friendships. Because she was also twenty years older, Jean decided to stop calling.

Moody and isolated, she decided to go back to group for awhile. The extreme problems of the women, overdrinking, lack of shelter, deep emotional problems, made Jean feel that she didn't belong. The group was built for women to support them from societal rejection. Some women, young as twenty, would rent a place for two; then three or four others would camp in there overnight. The money that a roof overhead cost was not looked at hard on, and the constant changing left many alone, emotionally and physically.

Jean recalled Miles telling her that it was the 'squeaky wheel that got the grease,' but Jean was so withdrawn that she could not extend herself, dealt with her introspection on her own, in her journal writing.

There was talk of another bunch soon to form, an offshoot of the support group; women of 'like' interests were being asked to join. But promise of a rise in consciousness was not fulfilled as women failed to show up at the first meeting.

Jean drifted back to the community once, but was turned off by the immensity of the problems. One woman broke out in tears over the fact that her husband had taken her two children away from her. Another related the story that six people had gotten involved in a fiction that her lover was dead or unconcious in an accident, a pure lie. Another was involved in college work and had read deeply into the Natalie Barney, Renee Vivian group of the 1920s. She was so intertwined in her second relationship that no one could break in to talk with her. Most of the support group soon became involved in a town music festival for the summer and worked far into the night over many beers. This wore down Jean's health.

Soon after this time, Jean continued to be withdrawn from the Drew and Eiko combination. In the one or two conversations Jean had with Drew, she became disgusted with her revelations of love... "She has a tendency to jabber in Spanish when excited," Drew referred to Eiko. Or... "Nobody could be my roommate because there are always clothes strewn all over the house." Jean gloomed around further. There is nothing so disgusting as relaying such intimate feelings to a bystander. You would have to be a post to convey real feeling.

Jean retreated much as a sedulous nun. Copy all my feelings into a notebook. Do my comfortable work. A retreat? Yes, there is nobody I can talk to. Outsider. First, I have to hear how an old love was lazy and drank up all her liquor. Then intimate details of how long, how big something was... how boring!

Better do something for yourself. Your own consciousness is sinking, not gaining. Bake some bread. Write, Yes, write. At least you have power that way over your own thinking. Most of those people will be dead or drunks in five years.

The next day Jean got up and called Kate. "Come on, you're free this holiday weekend, so am I. Can't you fly in to San Francisco? At least we can have some fun."

CHAPTER FOUR

When the Going Gets Weird

For a weekend they met in the Bay area. Spring was beginning again after a windy winter. Already the trees had a sign of bud; this was the time to make a plan, for what...a longer trip? Two estranged people reached out to alleviate that feeling of loneliness and alienation.

They were out on a six-hour drive of the city, late. Where did they go? They drove past the Presidio to Grace Slick's house. On the other side was a dark path through woods; they took it and strolled down the leaf-strewn path, taking the long view to the back of Golden Gate Bridge with orange lights marking the spot first entered by Cabrillo. Soundless, some trees rustling, not an intruder bothered them, and they were contentedly alone.

Heavenly to be together and not on a sexual tightrope. That factor doesn't enter in. Just a couple of good companions having fun, nothing to jeopardize a relationship. It keeps us on our up side mentally and physically.

They didn't see one car that night in the dark streets. They drove for hours through back streets, blissfully without stress. They drove through the canyons of the rich. The old San Francisco homes by the seacliffs, vine-covered, solid money mansions stayed lit even at four, where some solitary sat in a library.

Before their drive they had walked through the theater district around Geary and Union Square, past the ACT where *Morning's at Seven* was playing, sauntering past that theater and on to Broadway, blitzed with light. It made them think of Las Vegas.

Finally they closed in on a carnival atmosphere at the corner of Geary, a crazy scene. They saw a man and a woman, drunken, with the man holding a suitcase and a dress, holding the dress up to the lady as if to measure size, saying angrily... "All right, you go your way, and I'll go mine. Here is your half." And the man split the luggage into two piles. Instant divorce on a San Francisco street.

The next instant, as they walked ten steps across the street after this wild scene, they looked over their shoulders at the same corner to see "grandpa" clad only in his shorts. He had forgotten to put on his pants, and in the midnight air, very thin cotton shorts flapped against bare knees as he sailed cattycorner across the street, bewildered.

After a perfect weekend Jean and Kate returned, each to her work. Jean counseled herself, thinking...Yes, now. I have been pushing off the oldness. Maybe I should write about it.

FACING UP

I have been pushing off
Looking at the oldness
Now I counsel
Myself with the thought that
People don't care so much
About wrinkles; my wrinkles
Look and need the me
I can be when I am not hiding
When I let the me
Meet up with the world.
People want to talk about themselves,
Not my vainness or how wide
My waist is.
As I come out for a real meeting
So do they.
And, I feel a sense of relief
Talking about all this, but
I haven't really told you how my knees
Do ache in this rain, oh
Not a lot, and the pain isn't unbearable.
I am thickening in the ribcage in spite
Of all the exercise, running
One mile, and my weight training.
The wrinkles keep piling up around the eyes,
And nobody looks at me.

The next night, alone again, Jean woke at 4 a.m. from a nightmare in which she was being accused, back in the school district where she had taught, accused of being a lesbian. Officials at the school were looking at her picture in a room full of people, and they decided this pronouncement from the way she looked. Her hair was too blond and her eyes looked directly out. In this same dream she had her betrayers. Drew was the leader; she had admirers sitting on side kitchen steps behind a wooden door. They jeered at me... "Why don't you fight it?" On the outside of the door the general public was gathering and the president was preparing to take me to jail. Drew's bunch were saying, "Stand up for yourself!" But Jean's salary was to be cut and they were going to forbid her to teach. This was a convincing old war movie with Germans and Nazis. Jean awoke with a pain in her stomach, a gurgling, hurting spasm.

During the time before Jean and Kate were to be separated, the liaison continued, each hour filled. They took a day trip to Santa Monica pier to have fortunes told, ate salads always for slimming, shopping together. The time was spent as though to forestall thinking. There was no time alone then. And when one house came up for rent, one moved in with the other.

Jean's uneasiness remained. Why had she been selected? What commonality did they have? When the break did come, a devastation hit her, a polyp of pain stayed in her chest and her mind worked with the problem. She clung to her home all those months.

If I were a character in a book, she pondered, this would be a very gloomy chapter indeed.

CHAPTER FIVE

Llangolen by the Sea

Aha, now, the problem of living. How should we live? Do we have to live alone? Do people always leave us?

Jean was talking with Drew one day. "I see all kinds of women who live alone in their own houses or apartments. Why couldn't they get together in a project? They get together..."

"In meetings. Yeah. Why couldn't we..."

"Plan our own project..."

"With these people combined..."

"In their own studio..."

"Apartments or in a compound..."

"Have to have some kind of commonality..." murmured Jean.

"I'd have to have musicians of some kind. That's my whole life," insisted Drew.

"Your entire college work was music, wasn't it? And now..."

"Of course, but I do want a change..."

Drew responded, "Right now my stomach is hurting." She had a hand right below her bellybutton. "There's something wrong with this school system. I feel that way. I feel that the administration is chewing people up. After awhile the whole thing collapses. Right now there are three people around me sick, two women and one man, and I mean seriously sick. It's all a result of stress and feeling out of control of their lives. The people in authority are not treating the ones who do the work in a humane manner. So the pressure builds up. Some get a heart condition. Some get ulcers. And of course, some go bonkers sooner or later. I keep trying to avoid, but it doesn't work. It may take a few years, but the end result is, you get sick. I can feel it right now. I wish there'd be some place to find peace and comfort...I'd like to be heading in that direction where I could find beauty and create something, my own music, a place for women's music."

Jean looked at her. "I agree. The other day I went AWOL and went out and bought a canoe." She giggled at her release.

Drew went on, "Right now, I'm milling around, getting sick

many days, got hepatitis, staying out on sick days. We all get kinda scared, boxed in . . . I wish I . . ."

"Yes, I know," Jean completed her thought. "The other day they couldn't find me. You know where I was? I was sleeping in the stacks in the rare books room."

"Yeah, you just collapse. And we all have to work as a team, and you find when one part goes out, there's more work for the rest to do, and eventually everyone gets overloaded. Then nothing's any fun anymore. I wish I could change somehow, get out and create a new community, a good-spirited community, where we could enjoy each day and get some beauty into our lives."

"You aren't serious?"

"But I *am* serious."

Jean really thought about it the next week. She met with the most business-minded of their group, Carolyn, who had amassed a fortune in apartment units. Carolyn was practical. Maybe she could see a way to reality that was more than dreaming.

Jean quizzed her, "Do you know that place in the California Piedmont, close to the coast, around one hundred miles away?"

"Yeah, of course. So?"

"Couldn't something be done with that? The existing buildings seem to fit the idea. You remember those white-walled buildings, Tudor, kind of English or Welsh?"

"Yeah, but some religious group owns that," objected Carolyn.

"We could make them an offer. Maybe they've outgrown it. If you ask me; it looks deserted in some respects."

"I don't mind taking a look at it, but I don't want to set out a lot of personal money on it." Carolyn was wary, uninvolved.

"No, but maybe some kind of loan from the state for a co-op perhaps."

"The thing would have to be fixed up, maybe rezone."

"I know, but will you come with me one day?" Jean kept on.

"OK, I've heard of some places getting grants or loans to make co-ops before. I could see if it's worth it."

Jean persisted with her idea . . . "Do you think they might sell?"

Carolyn was reluctant to say. "Have to have financing."

"It's true, you get one person to finance; the units could be purchased then individually."

"You think it's been done before, sort of a co-op?" Jean was eager.

"As I say, we'd have to see. Don't count too heavily on it."

"Then can you come look?" Jean went on.

Carolyn said, "Yep." Then she closed her mouth and Jean knew better than to keep at it.

At another party, Jean reopened the subject. "You could live there too. People could all eat together and then retreat to their own cottage at night. We could call it 'Llangolen West' after the ladies in Wales who used to knit bluestockings while waiting for their literary friends to come to visit them."

Carolyn looked at her coldly. "What kind of people would move clear over there?"

"Lots of people. Our friends. You'd be a help and they are interesting. One woman I know is a journeyman electrician. I don't know any plumbers, but we could hire that. Each woman who bought could change her own unit and finish it the way she wanted to."

"I only say I'll look at it with you. I don't jeopardize myself. I pay only ten percent down on properties." But Carolyn agreed to come with her.

Jean thought more on it when she got home alone. It wasn't hard to find solitary women. Many lived four to a house because they had to to survive. Thinking about this made her happy. If I had a small place to put essential books, a kitchen, a bed alcove, I'd gladly sell off what I have here.

Wandering thoughts about essentials occupied her. People could eat in the dining hall, and after the beef bourguignon, tossed salad and Danish bread, they could return to their own units for coffee. She fantasized further in the next two months. What details would come into play? Would they include men? They had a friend named Hans who could be perfect for an innkeeper. He had a German girlfriend who would have to come with him. People could have one pet; some partnerships were allowed. A plan whereby the place could be resold would have to be worked through.

Carolyn came through and together they walked over the compound, seeing the church ownership the next afternoon. It turned out that the place was for sale. Carolyn puzzled herself with the money it would cost.

The first woman agreeing to plunk down money was Drew. She had been lead singer and guitar player in a band that had played for a year and a half on weekends. She was interested in giving music training, harmony and theory classes. She came over to the spot with Carolyn who was sizing it up with an eye to financial cost.

During the speculation period the fog came in on time; dripping trees left sticky substances on the pavement, while the rising wind increased the chilled coastal air.

"Enough to dampen my feeling of possibility," grumbled Carolyn, who had promised to look into the project. She had filled out an initial statement to a church group. She also began work with some L.A. financial institution.

While Carolyn was looking at the outside, a workman came up in a Ford van with his golden retriever, waiting to fix the plumbing.

Hmm . . . that's ok to have a man come in. None of the others we know can do it. We have a potential electrician, Nellie, and friend Marsha and five-year-old Jack; they're going to be a unit. If they come in, they want to do up a unit with Marsha's big library, make a bookstore and add books from book outlets up north. It's a start, has a potential. Carolyn didn't think bookstores made money, however. Maybe they can make it by being a meeting house, collecting fees.

Drew was the one with the most enthusiasm.

"Are you sure, Drew, about going through with this?" Jean was back on a surface level with her.

Drew wasn't deterred by the dank weather or any other obstacle. "Sure. I'm sick of my old life. I like to do things after I've made up my mind. I know a lot of women who'll come in on this. I also like the climate."

"Which unit? You'd have first choice of living quarters."

"I'd like the place which might be on top of the bookstore; its got a bedroom, kitchen and sofa space. I also know a couple who have said they'd like to buy in down the back side, where the stairs climb up the cliff."

"With money?"

"Yes, they have enough money. And we do need a constant

caretaker, a pub keeper like in England."

Jean filled in with Hans. "He has a friendly personality, a host perhaps, and Gretyl can bake. They could go in the first place, greet people, and schedule the workshops that would take place in 'Longshed.' All notices could go there. Most of the units..."

"Are small..."

"But sometimes two people could squeeze in..."

"I want all the rest to be music people, except for Bearcat Bookstore; we could have that for small recitals."

"What about me? I'm not music." Jean was concerned with the problem. They never could see eye to eye; communication was hard. They never discussed books; the conversation dropped.

"Yes, you. Well, you're invited," guffawed Drew.

The sky now pewter gray, a heavy fog covered the entire valley beyond the Piedmont, and the Pacific was only a smudge to the west. Even though the winter solstice had passed, the entire coast down the long vee that marked the town was covered in winter gloom. As Carolyn left the row of cottages to return home, she drove into a chillier valley, and the smutty air made her worry.

"People are all closed up like mussels on rocks. Will enough go along with this phantom scheme?"

"It's soon going to be spring," Jean encouraged her. "Now, while everybody's holed up, we can lay down our plans. When better weather hits..."

"We'll be ready for other buyers and..."

"What are you...?"

"Let's approach that innkeeper first. He's practical and I'm certainly practical." Carolyn was thinking it through.

"In the meantime?"

"Let's line up a man who does drywall who is fast at fixing, and also find out if we have to contact the Coastal Commission."

"Well, if you're thinking like that, maybe I can get George to restructure Longshed; it could be longer."

They headed into the city, rain clouds at their car windows. In colder parts of the country, weathermen spoke of minus 85 degrees. But in the desert city they re-entered, a smoky pall fell into dusk and early night. Their heads were so full of promising plans they forgot they were supposed to be depressed. This plan shaping up, of having a centralized place for people in music and for all women's music, tantalized Drew. The idea lay like a dormant chrysallis in the cocoon of Llangolen West.

CHAPTER SIX

Creating a Composition

Soon to be the Directress of a new music school, Drew cast about for ways to cut off old ties, get relocated. She had her friend who lived in another house. Presumably, Eiko would come with her. She could be relied upon for many things. Drew told few about her plans; she was competently making her next move. In addition, she was becoming more physically active, running a long jogging course with Eiko, and leaving heavy drinking parties out of her life.

The next development was to sell the house she had lived in for a long time and buy the individual unit with the profit. In addition, she would make the change in her life that she had wanted. Why not start a school for women and girls who played music and do her teaching there? The thing had been done in Greece some 2600 years ago by Sappho, but had not been repeated.

In Drew's case it was possible, because she had her Master's degree in music. She could teach, could inspire others to join the staff. The idea gained in strength as the winter wore on and storms hurled rains to green up grazing lands in the hills around Llangolen. The school, and what it was to be, became a conscious part of the women's talk. Some went to view the property. Others scraped up down payments.

Carolyn went off to a central bank, Jean alongside, and they found out the purchase was possible. A banker friend helped them to acquire the property. Their idea came closer to fact!

Drew was the first to buy a unit. Along with her was her friend Eiko, who could give flute lessons. The plan was now expanded to include having a women's night of music at the site, with the participants spread out in camping areas on the embankment.

Within a month Drew closed her escrow and was able to go into her unit, hauling in her musical decor. She had the walls plastered and got some tubas for bases on the tables and standing lamps in the form of piccolos. Her stereo system was installed over one weekend; this was a $3,000 unit which dominated the entire wall overhead.

As soon as Drew was in, Carolyn fitted out the second unit. After a month and a half, her cottage was starkly modern, with luxurious sofas and tables, pop art on the walls, and a lot of chrome. She installed the best of bedding in each of her two bedrooms.

As for Jean, the third of the triumvirate, she was located in a loft apartment. To get to her bedroom one had to climb a circular staircase of wrought iron, painted white, rising along white walls which contained one Manet and one Matisse. As the staircase rounded the alcove, one could see that the double bed was covered with a Norwegian dyner, down comforter, cased in light blue flowers, and at the head, many blue pillows. A trough full of twelve books, new books from Pandora, a Louise Bogan poetry book and Sarton were in this. At a windowsill rested a simple white clay pot filled with nasturtiums.

Downstairs, two walls were painted white, others held only books. Books were scattered on all the chairs; Collette, Stein, Jean Rhys, all lusty and strange, were arranged in groups, while on the desk were Sackville-West and Steinem, Robin Morgan, Violette Leduc. A person was allowed to borrow books, as long as one left one's Bankamericard. She had a crook lamp bent over a Morris chair.

There was a corduroy seat filling the bay window, while to the south a sunporch was framed in bamboo curtains. The typewriter stood on a table, with a blue pneumatically operated secretary's chair. On the top of another teak desk stood a single Sung vase with one blue hydrangea.

CHAPTER SEVEN

Anger and Remorse

Drew was sitting in the middle of the front porch of the bookstore. She had had a hard night at the Pelican Inn. The flooring of the bookstore wasn't yet done, and shavings littered the floor. The dream was coming into reality.

Inside the open door the room was irradiated from the stained glass prisms lining one window. Drew was contemplating her little boy boots which she stretched in front of her. Nothing was moving. On a plasterer's sawhorse stood a cold bottle of Perrier. The night before had left her hung over and unable to think. In the driveway outside the white buildings there wasn't a car.

Finally a plumbing truck pulled up and a boy of nineteen got out, swinging his leather bag of metal tools. He went in a door, but nobody was up so he returned to his truck and left. All was still for a time; during that period Drew shifted position once. Finally she got up and returned with a small can of ale which she rested at her feet.

Drew's face was cleanly without makeup in the morning sun. Even after a late night her face was seductively beautiful as she headed toward the thirty-fifth year, when American women seem to peak. Her hair in light brown tawny shades made a cap around her face. In a silky cotton white blouse and brown corduroys tucked into her boots, she looked like a Cossack princess or a New York model.

Eleven o'clock came. The same truck reappeared, and this time the boy went into one of the doors. Another door opened and the innkeeper came out in his shirt sleeves, yawning at the wintery sunlight.

Drew had not been alone that night. Inside the unfinished bookstore, beyond the showcases and sawhorses, the door to her bedroom showed a tumbled heap of bedclothes. Here also was a stack of records and a photo mock-up of the summer music festival. From time to time her friend Eiko was there overnight, but sometimes she went to the Long Beach area.

Finally at twelve a phone rang in the next house. Dorothea, one of the new owners, came out to ask her if she would like to come.

"Come to where?"

"Come to help these people at the beach," Dorothea went on. "They had a big party in that square boxcar at the end. It was a disaster. Cassie and Lori got into a mean fight over something, terribly mad. Cassie swung at Lori and a beer bottle got broken. Anyhow, somehow, Cassie poked that bottle into Lori's eye and there is blood everywhere."

"Why do they want me?"

"They think you can help. Can you come to take her to the hospital? They can't find the key to their car, and nobody's doing anything to help Lori."

Dorothea disappeared into her house, and Drew got up slowly, returned to her bed alcove and turned off the stereo. She washed her face heavily with soap, pulled on some formal pants, and found her wallet. Outside she eased into the four-wheel drive GMC truck filled with lumber and backed slowly out the drive.

Had her life always been like this? Yes, someone was always calling her to pick up the pieces from some disaster, go find somebody.

Drew returned to the compound four or five hours later, about dusk.

"Everything all right?"

"No." Drew lowered her feet to the ground. "No, not all right. She's lost an eye. They're keeping her at St. Francis for a week. It's so swollen they are not positive at this point."

"What does she say happened?" Jean pursued the accident.

"She says she didn't know she could get that mad," returned Drew. "Right now they, well, Cassie is in a state of shock. They've got Lori under sedatives, heavy; she's not aware of the eye."

Drew eased her long legs out of the truck and walked into the sawdust on the floor of the bookstore. She wished she had someone to be the strong one once in awhile, decide what to do. Eiko was gone most of the time. She wished she had a little support. Inside she found the microwave in the back kitchen alcove. She put some croissants and ham on a plate and heated up a cup of coffee. Then she sat down tiredly at her polished oak table.

CHAPTER EIGHT

Music Festival Advance

On the next Saturday in late March, a few cars began gathering. They were there for the weekend to meet about the summer Music Festival. Some were in ordinary work shirts, some carried out sacks of foodstuffs. The cars were old, heavy Buicks and Lincolns. A few ancient Volkswagons with encrusted dust sputtered up the drive and five young women got out. They took signs into the long shed meeting house. They were getting ready for the time when a thousand people from all over California would have to be housed.

Carolyn had arranged with her staff of moonlighters for canvas tarps and outdoor sanitation. She and Jean had a discussion over the state of purchase of the units.

"We think it's getting complete." Jean was enthusiastic. "What is left is only one crafts house or practice room about 20 by 30 feet, and there are three dorm rooms above the eating hall. Otherwise all the units have been bought up . . ."

"I know, I know," Carolyn added. "I'm able to cover the loan payment; the strain is over. I just have to front one-third of the total."

"Drew is all settled in the new music school. What happened to her old job?"

"I don't know how she got out of it; she doesn't tell," Jean added. "What I do know is that she is lined up with a band to go to New Orleans for a week and then has a three-day engagement in Houston. That'll be over with about a week before the festival gets underway."

"Has she said Eiko is going with her?" Carolyn pressed on.

"Don't know; Eiko is around, but there are some others too. I don't have Drew's ear at all any more, not since the holidays."

Jean walked back to her own cottage. She brooded over the price she had to pay to gain communication. This was better than being totally alone. Still, it led to the warped view that everybody else was happy with their mates, going through halcyon days, funning together, sharing a movie. She thought she was singular; her friends didn't know what to do to help her. The thoughts of others' lives going perfectly was really erroneous, because some of them had enormous business debt; some were pulled to a rag by long working days. The ecstasy she imagined was only imagination. Not too bad, she thought, solitariness, once I get into it. Actually I like it. The phone rang once and then stopped.

Drew had arranged at this time to leave Jean in charge of the compound to organize the summer festival; then she took off in this post-Mardi Gras time to New Orleans. The trip was taken in the blue GMC van which Drew had fitted out to sleeping space. The rest of the band was in another car and they met twice, once in Houston and once in San Antonio. When they drove into the main section of New Orleans, Drew's group went in to claim a room at the new Iberville, right off the main part of Canal Street. The others took a private hotel in the French Quarter. The revels of Bacchus had died down and the people were celebrating Lent; this didn't prevent the bars being open all night long, tired jazz coming out of the corner Dixieland hotspots. Crowds still roamed all night down Bourbon Street with their Hurricane cups, and the streets were awash with beer.

Drew parked the van in the lot along Canal Street. The three of them entered a marbled foyer on the ground floor and took a glass outside elevator. An open gridwork of white metal loomed over their heads; it had an Ice Palace of 1900 look. Seven tiers of hanging plants disappeared below them as they went up.

On the top floor of the plush Iberville they stepped into a sumptuous reception and desk section. They could hear a 1940s swing band playing "Poor Butterfly." This attracted a certain moneyed crowd, affluent, yet not truly rich. People who were on their way up, who liked "show," wanted to be seen at the best hostelry in town.

On the dance floor a man in his 60s, white mustached, danced with a decorous matron. The people were pleasantly satisfied with themselves.

Drew and the rest of the band stumbled in, trying to get their rooms. They were frazzled from being on the road all night from Houston.

They found the desk as "After You've Gone" swelled up after the "Butterfly" number. Drew winced and looked around, winked and said, "You'll never catch me out there, ever."

Interior walls were covered with panels of cherrywood which rose over four elevator doors, brass on the doors themselves, bounded by Roman arches. The potted palms surrounded the steps which rose to the dining area. On the far wall a twenty-foot medieval tapestry faced them. The main sitting area held several silky teal overstuffed loveseats and long low chairs built for heavy people. One table held a fresh spring bouquet of snapdragons and yellow tiger lilies in a crystal bowl.

As Drew, Eiko and the others sank into the soft seats which overlooked the harbor, a hostess in proper low black shoes, with black hose and silky white blouse streaked with satin stripes, asked for their orders. They settled on Bloody Marys.

Most of the people were dressed casually. Drew picked up her glass. "Well, here's to New Orleans; hope they can take our rock. Do you think we fit in?"

Below, the Bienville Street wharf edged the Mississippi. Orange and black tankers pushed slowly toward the warehouses which were gaudily red and yellow. It made a colorful scene from the cherrywood interior.

"Let's get down to the real place, the Quarter, and see Bourbon Street before we crash. Why don't all of you park your stuff in our room, change a blouse and go?"

Once in the Quarter, they drove to the small hotel where the rest were to stay, Eiko among them. Drew said, "Where did Alicia go? I think I can count on her to give me a line of coke."

They passed the late afternoon and evening in one of the old bars of the section, staring out from the patio into the grilled park. Eiko was appearing and then disappearing with a new gang, and the rest finally ambled around the streets, taking all drinks from bar to bar. Drew was due at the club where they were to play at 9:30, and from that time on Drew was never sure of where anybody was for the next eight days. The night life went on till six in the morning. Many bars had not been closed in generations.

After their set they milled around in the crowd, getting steadily drunker. They were there after Mardi Gras, but still there was pandemonium. Several times Drew was accosted by a hostile voice, "What are you, anyway, a boy or a girl?" Eiko pushed Drew to one side, out into the middle of the street. "Come on, we don't want to get into that; they're ready to fight. And for God's sake, don't say faggot; they'll knock your block off."

The next night they found themselves close to the levee by the Mississippi, one block from Canal Street. They had a run-in with a gang of teenagers. At this point they had to hold up Drew. "Let's throw her in."

The Mississippi washed its gray waves against the paving blocks which marked the levee.

"Let's take her jeans off."

They took her corduroy pants off and left them by the levee.

Then they all staggered off toward the smooth front of the Iberville; they all piled into the glass elevators where there was no attendant.

"Here, let's climb on those white guard rails at the top of the open air pavilion."

"No, you go."

Then the elevator stopped and disgorged them into the dining area.

"Here, cover her up. Climb up those steps and get a tablecloth."

They ripped a tablecover, dislodging glassware with a tinkling sound, wrapped this around Drew and bundled her up to their room. They were not unnoticed by the bellhops. Inside the room, the eight of them went on with their party, finally falling asleep for an hour. Then, the wildness of the party distressing the management, they were thrown out of the room. Here they found that Drew was in no condition to drive the van. One of the others signed an enormous bill for damages, and then they headed off toward Rampart Street. Drew was stuck with the bill.

Meanwhile, Jean, back at Llangolen, telephoned a few times, but was unable to make sense out of their conversations. Most of them were able to do some tourist things in the afternoons. Three of them took a cemetary tour in the old burial grounds of New Orleans; these are so markedly different because the dead have to be buried in above-ground vaults. The tombs have to be renovated to make way for the newer generations. All the bones have to be dug up, the dry dirt and mementos sifted, and new stone markers erected.All of New Orleans is below sea level. If this renovation didn't take place, the decomposed bodies would wash up into the streets. The tombs themselves were interesting-looking, but sometimes the graveyards were not safe places to go.

Another group made it upstate in Louisiana to go to the great swamp, the Atchefayala. Here they saw the start of spring coming through the bare branches and swampy canebrakes. Flowers were starting their blooming luxuriance. In an old pirogue a dummy of a Cajun fisherman caught their eye. They toured the swamp with a Cajun guide, observing overhead the girders supporting the I-10, which ran through the state. Later they ate in the run-down-looking "Chez Nous," famous for its Cajun gumbo with shrimp and chicken and red sauce. Each tried crawfish stew with red beans and rice, ending their feast with bread pudding.

For the most part, Drew and the band slept through the warm afternoons, getting drunker and shakier. They would be sodden with sleep and red-eyed, sick as if to die, and then the music outside their window would start up again; they'd rise up and say, "Hey, it's time to go out." This went on for six days and seven nights. Suddenly, one night after the band had folded up their instruments, Drew said to Eiko, whom she hadn't seen for three nights, "What day is this?"

Most of them had been drunk for six nights, Drew having complicated things with some drugs. They decided they had to get her back to the West and some sanity. They put four people in the van to go back across the country. Drew decided to go by plane, and Eiko gave her a last supply of coke. Eiko then disappeared. Drew didn't see her again until a week in the mid-summer music festival.

Early the final morning they all gathered at the Cafe du Monde for the famous coffee of New Orleans. Strong, black, laced with chicory and steamed milk, it was poured from boiling vats which lined the counter. Drew guided them toward a big table of affluent young people, lounging after an overnight spree. These youngsters from the rich mansions on Garden Street moved out insolently, and Drew could sit down. The table was covered with powdered sugar from the beignets, a French doughnut.

Everyone was in a colorful costume. The white-aproned waiters served the creamy light brown mixture and set down heaping plates of the doughnuts covered with sugar. They would never forget the beignet experience.

Looking about them at the street, Drew felt they were in a kind of medieval fair about to begin. The green canvasses surrounding the cafe were half lowered. It was like being at an early morning horse race or produce market. The mist came in from the marshy river embankment and obscured the iron grillwork of the square.

After the breakfast they loaded up their duffle bags and headed toward the hotel where they were to catch a bus to the airport. The dreamy quality of the streets, the ballustrades shrouded in mist, gave the sense of decay of old wood, sea-drenched buildings, passage of countless generations. No other city has that flavor.

They boarded their airplane, Drew without Eiko and her drug supply. She was in an agitated, frenetic state when they landed in Los Angeles. A sense of hopelessness, unconscious of the others, hung over her like the mist. In a state of nervous collapse, Drew reentered the state of California.

She was present in body during the week-long festival, but she was not functioning. Thus her leadership was found wanting and Jean and the others had to run all activities.

After the New Orleans trip the entire music festival planning went along rapidly. Everyone at Llangolen was completely involved, particularly Jean, who was pulling all the strings together from her top apartment, especially as it seemed that Drew was being ineffective. Eiko reappeared two weeks after the trip; she had two strangers with her and they all slept in Drew's apartment. Many newcomers kept coming and going from Drew's bedroom, climbing from the stairs above the Bearcat Bookstore. Jean was never sure what was going on there.

She attended to her duties, arranging with a construction company in town for the outhouses. The upstairs dormitory rooms located above the dining hall were converted into wall-to-wall sleeping cubicles with inflatable mattresses. A local contractor bulldozed sites on the hillside, forming bench niches for the camping spots. The amphitheater was the setting for the week-long performances.

These details she attended to. Jean had no time for herself; and yet, even if she had, she had nobody to converse with. During the evening she was usually quiet in her bedroom under the eaves. The checked squares of a handmade quilt, blue and white cornflowers in small stitching, rested on a high-backed chair. In the mornings a cool breeze came through the half-opened window, wafting the orange heads of the nasturtiums in the window box. Her room was serene.

She wished it weren't quite that peaceful. She knew that loneliness usually stops after awhile. Something pops up. Drew had always been an alleviation in the past. The friendship hadn't had a sharp role since they were trying to figure out what they had to give each other. Intelligence and feminism. Musicianship couldn't come into the picture, and sometimes she thought only musicians could talk to other musicians. Jean thought it was Drew's sureness that drew people to her. She had a sense of accuracy that kept her on top of things. But lately Drew was so scattered. Perhaps there was something wrong with her.

Down Jean's stairs and to the right, Drew's apartment was alive with people, driving in and out the driveway in Drew's van, while Drew, her hands waving around, appeared to be the host of an unending party. Jean thought that when there were a lot of people coming and going for short periods there had to be drugs involved.

Jean could never see when Drew slept. She rarely completed a sentence. Sometimes she just stared blankly. At times she would be drunk all day, then, just when the meeting was supposed to start, she went to bed.

Yet the brochures had been readied by somebody in the group; Jean had secured enough rooms for accommodation, the publicity was out for a major entertainer, and twelve bands were to come on July 12 through the 18th. Somebody in Drew's entourage was working effectively, if only in spasms.

When Drew wasn't up, the rest of the compound was busily at work. One day she did appear at her doorway, a Panthia reactivated in a 1980s version of the perfect Ionian statue, fairest of women, with strong blue eyes, fair brows, and a bronze blonde skullcap making her the epitome of a young Greek beauty. But she leaned against the doorway, sagged, and then went back to bed.

Jean was half afraid of her too, her ability to turn and ignore; sometimes she would plan a hurtful trick, calculated to sting. Luckily some wickedly contrived plan misfired, or slipped by the target. Already several in the compound were wary of Drew. For that reason Jean also found herself avoiding her. She finally resorted to little or no contact with Drew. The age difference seemed to be cropping up a lot now.

Jean thought about some of the past activities where they had shared some fun. She felt the twenty years yawning like a canyon. There was little hope of throwing a rope across it. Sometimes she felt like a grandma with no offspring. She knew she had never wanted children, though. She had enough to do in pursuing her own career.

Nightly drinking bouts upset the routine. The people hanging around Drew were usually up in her bedroom and they were always stoned. Or they were taking something else. Gretyl had to watch the two children who belonged to two of the women involved in the group. By that time at night there was a certain drift from the planning. Nothing was said directly to Jean, but she found herself an outsider, unable to keep up the "drunk all night, up in the morning" routine. She had to tell them so.

Jean made her own discipline, up early in the morning, running and jogging, lifting weights at the gym, swimming three days a week. The small town was accommodating to fitness; many of the women ran half marathons. Still, she found herself unable to keep pace with the younger women.

There! I know. Zap them when they got patronizing. No wonder Virginia Woolf was mean and cutting to young women. Virginia understood how the odds were in their favor, and thought to attack them first. Why not wise up, she thought. Be like Virginia who could be unmerciful to youngsters, especially those who were badly educated. She would draw them out about their uninformed view of current news and then expose them sharply and bitingly with her own analytical mind. They would be pinned by her wit. "What do you mean the day was fine? Was it a red sunrise or a yellow? Did the cartman sing as he brought you along?" And she would befuddle them with her cross-examination, leaving them rosy and feeling a fool. Why don't you try that tack? Jean corrected her own passivity.

The weekend of the festival bore down on them. A hillside of camptown women arrived, most of them from the North and other states. Jean, together with Michelle and Hans got them located for the first night, but the food situation raised problems because many of the northern group would eat only health food, and the L.A. women only kosher-prepared. Still, the first official performance found all the women in the midst of the wailing tenor of jazz and the hot horn of Tiny Davis. A blues group with a Nashville influence sang through a mix of soft ballad and folk tunes. "Out of the Blues" was sung. They all went to bed that night knowing that the festival had started. It was a success.

During the week Jean scarcely had time to think. She fielded one problem after another, mostly easy ones. Somehow, the compound hung together and the town accommodated itself to blasts of acoustic guitar. The country music alternated with blues and jazz. There was a major argument over racial discrimination when it was found that the kitchen workers were black, which had to be disclaimed. The first year's major effort finally skidded to a halt on a Sunday night.

Jean slumped over her desk on the south sunporch. She was exhausted. They had all pulled the same direction. Everyone finished intact. But Drew was acting cranky with some new drug. She gave unreasonable requests that forced others to do as they were told, and her eyes looked so wild that they did what she said. As all of them afterward agreed, there was something wrong with Drew.

CHAPTER NINE

A Physical Collapse

Drew was in a nervous state after the festival people left; she could not sleep for three nights and four days. Incoherent when she spoke with the others, she didn't comb her hair or wash her face. She seemed oblivious to all the others, and when Jean would ask her to do something she would stare at her with eyes cold as aquamarines. She kept asking where Eiko had gone, but Eiko had not been around since New Orleans. Most nights Drew continued to party with her friends and wave her arms around, being the life of the compound, but Jean observed she never seemed to eat, and she made fun of the others when they sat down at the long shed dining table. Her funny remarks were becoming more barbed and cruel.

A telling step of her deterioration came when she snarled out an angry retort to Hans and Jean and, getting into her GMC, accelerated backwards into a brick wall. She was frenzied, brilliant, and yet, terribly unreasonable. A hostile destructiveness in a bar downtown forced the owners to call the police. One night the patrol car drove her up to the compound and the officer suggested that they get some professional help.

Finally, after some consultation, Jean and Michelle took her to the hospital. From there the drug abuse people suggested sending her to Kaylor Center for observation and rehabilitation. She remained for two months. She had to go through a withdrawal period, then was given medication and psychiatric help.

While she was at the Center, the other women at Llangolen West pursued their business of getting the school to run. The eternal party above the bookstore stopped. The Bearcat Bookstore was doing a steady business, but they still weren't making a living at it. Twice a week different groups met in the building; poetry sessions, string quartet performances, and professional music conferences went on.

Gradually the school setting grew. Some of the musicians, a cellist, two violinists, a flute player, two pianists were practicing four hours a day; also, the lessons went on. The conservatory in the main building was growing in numbers of practice rooms, and some townspeople were now paying tuition.

The idea of having a music school for women was a vision in their minds, but so far, the reality had not been accomplished. They all missed Drew, for somehow she had emerged as the focus, the energy. She had been the one who felt sharpest the repression of the school system, the pushing down to mediocrity. She had the force of a heroine, and could not be held back too long. This was her break-away period, and the image in her mind was not to be suppressed. September came along, the beginning of the truly fine weather.

Hardest hit was Jean. She grieved for her lost friendship, as Drew was constantly in the company of Eiko. She rarely spoke to any of the others, including Jean; it was as if she had never known her. The others biked together, ran together, and, as it turned out, were doing a lot of drugs together. It had been an abrupt slap. Jean retreated. She blamed herself, her square character. She was too quiet, too passive, she reasoned, yes, and too staid. She was stuck in the sixties. She resumed her habit of daily journal writing and poured her wounds into it.

Somehow, she thought, talking into this journal helps me interpret what has been happening to me. It isn't reporting a life. She seemed to be always a bystander to life. But she needed to put sense to the passage of time and what was happening to them. She started to get tense and hunched her shoulders as if in protection against Drew and her friends. As Drew got higher, Jean felt stressed and felt inadequate. Drew had been constantly 'on stage,' but she hadn't noticed the deterioration and erratic conditions around her. She was fun, but then she wouldn't come out for days, having been in one of her 'moods.'

Jean and Michelle were planning a trip to Kaylor Medical Center to visit Drew. The school had been open six months.

"I hope she's better," broke out Michelle. "She was running around so much she didn't have time for running an embryo music school."

"Yeah, well Eiko was very much in evidence back then,"

reminded Jean.

"I know, and now we haven't seen her in three weeks. I wonder what happened to her. I think she was the Colombian connection. Where'd she go, back to Colombia?"

"She hasn't been here since the festival. I think Drew was probably looking for a new friend."

Indeed, Drew was restless, wishing she had a close friend who could be strong for her at times. Drew usually never did things on impulse. That was what troubled the other project leaders; they minded losing her sense of direction. It would be good for them all if Drew could find some deep-bosomed woman to keep her interest, some throwback to heroic Greece. Drew was in search of the right person, someone who could share her music.

Several times they went to see Drew at Kaylor.

"Drew," Michelle began, "we need you back in Llangolen. How are you making it here?"

Drew looked normal, but the authorities in charge of her case had her mind covered with some sedating, mind-altering drugs, two or three kinds. She had to take pills three times daily.

"I'm sleeping; in fact, too much. I go to bed by ten, then don't wake up until seven-thirty. They put us through drug therapy talk-out sessions in the afternoons. We go to group."

"Aren't you playing any music?"

"No, there's no chance. We exercise about three hours. They keep us busy all day. I started a jogging program, about a mile, and I'm thinking about getting a bike."

"How do you have to work around here?"

"Mainly I have to take care of myself, make my bed, eat breakfast on time, wash my clothes. It all has to be done by nine o'clock. The first exercise class starts then."

"How do you feel about coming home?"

"Heck, of course I'm missing all of you. They're trying to get me ready so I can be independently at home, but not too tempted by my own routine. They think I might be ready if I had a place to stay; anyhow, pretty soon. By the way, have you seen Eiko?"

"We haven't, except that last time right after the festival."

"The thing I last remember was being in New Orleans."

"Do you remember flying home from New Orleans?" Michelle

was testing her.

"Nope, none of that. Say, could you come next time with some goodies, some fruit or some celery or fresh stuff? The food's good, but it's mainly meat and potatoes. Maybe a package of cookies?"

Drew looked good, but her eyes were dull and she didn't look at them directly, but out of the corners. Still, her beauty was arresting. She was sitting in her hospital gown, which was designed like a Greek peplos, that loose-fitting garment worn by girls in ancient times. The one-piece tunic lay bare at the bottom, displaying a gleaming thigh. Running had made her fit, and she certainly hadn't gained weight on the institution food.

Frowning a little, she drew her mind to their problem.

Pleased at her concentration, Jean put the worry out afresh. "Drew, we definitely need your leadership. None of us seem to have what you have. This place is going, but it doesn't have a gyroscope. The school is running, maintaining itself, but we are not sure about the tuition. Should we give scholarships or a free ride to anyone? This whole thing will go stale and become just another hare-brained scheme. Put yourself together to manage us."

There. It was out. And plain. Even they had not been able to put it in words before.

Drew seemed to attach her mind to their problems; then went off into her own thoughts. Her blue eyes went unfocused. Her only remark as they left was... "Wonder if my conservator will give me money for a new cowboy hat. I only get so much a week."

On the long drive back Michelle said, "She looks good on the outside. Maybe she can get out soon. Maybe by late September...."

But Jean frowned as if in doubt.

CHAPTER TEN

New Directions

The new enrollment for general schooling was to start in mid-September. The Pacific fall weather of the upper Central Coast was sparkling; glints of sunlight on the blue waters below the cliffs gave the aura of Grecian tranquility to California. The true magical music school was almost within their grasp.

Jean thought over the eight months since the beginning. She was riding with Michelle up the long five miles out of Llangolen to a berry farm which sold home-baked chicken pies.

"Remember when the project was first purchased? Carolyn came up with the multi-million dollar loan from down south. We got that far. It has been commercially feasible..."

"Not only that. We have installed people in there. Twelve units have been bought...."

"Anything written down that says we can't sell when we want to?"

"You don't want to sell, do you? No, I thought not. No, the rules are very relaxed. If you want to go, you simply find another buyer, same as any other real estate."

"Good. Well, we've started. And a conservatory is started. What we want is our leader back."

"Yeah, to hector us into more action. Maybe we ought to badger her into getting well. We miss her leadership, that's certain."

At the driveway to the compound, Jean pulled up to Drew's apartment and there, to her surprise, Eiko was coming out. Other women were with her. They all had coiled cotton bands around their heads, after the manner of Japanese artisans, and their pants and shirts were tattered.

Eiko looked over at Jean briefly and then said sullenly, "Hi. Where did Drew go?"

"Hi, Eiko," and Jean thought, "How come she's still got the key to Drew's place?"

"She's in the hospital, been sick. Didn't you know?"

"I just got back from L.A. Say, you don't know where we could get something to eat?" She waved her hand back at her three companions and didn't act concerned at all about Drew.

Jean directed them down the road to a smorgasbord place. This development probably meant that the connection was broken. As it happened, Eiko's return coincided with the long-awaited re-entry of Drew to the compound. When they returned from eating, Drew came in and there was a sharp exchange, one volley between them, and then it was over. Eiko and the rest of her friends headed for San Diego. Jean did not see Eiko again. She reflected to herself that Drew had been shuffling her feet in one place all through the turmoil with late nights and the crazy drinking and drugging that little band had been doing. It had not only left Jean and Hans and Michelle alienated, but had left no room for accomplishment at the school. But now, perhaps, that wishing to have fun all the time would be diverted.

* * *

As Drew and Jean and Michelle, the two friends who had nursed her through her physiological collapse, drove slowly through the long approach to Llangolen, the village sparked up new interest. Crisp fall weather had changed the jacaranda leaves which lined the streets, and down the western part of town a glimpse of bright ocean lay beyond. About a dozen additional stores stretched down the road, one in French Normandy wood and stucco, the rest in English style. Llangolen gave a strong hint of western England and Wales. Behind the store which specialized in toy soldiers jutted up a straw-thatched house where the toy store owners lived. Llangolen was cool like western England.

On the south side of town below the main street, a new chain of low buildings housed a writers' guild, a West Coast MacDowell Institute. Here in cubicles were housed deserving writers from the rest of the country. The influx of talent was changing the town.

Drew asked who was new and of interest, and as Jean related and sketched out the people she had heard of who were currently in the colony, Drew seemed to be following. Jean thought she seemed to have a lot of mental energy. She seemed happy and remarked how the village seemed enchanted.

"You know, I feel right. This is the time for me to be here. I don't think I'm left with any residue, just know I have to work and make every hour count for something. I think I'm clean and won't want to be using anything, because I want our music school to work. We should find a few people as MacDowell does."

Jean wasn't sure about the music they would be having. "What kinds of lessons?"

"We'll have regular classes, college-level, harmony classes, theory, with world-renowned teachers."

Jean returned to the practical. "We have one unit solidly entrenched now. Everybody's paying mortgages. Some people are sharing housing until they find space in town."

"What kind of publicity has it been getting?"

"Drew, we've got some national attention now."

"Is it just word of mouth, or have you been getting news stories?"

"There've been articles printed about this western music school."

"I need to get back to reality." Drew was thoughtful. "Need to shape the development."

"You're so right. Most of the rest of us are busy just trying to develop our own places."

As they turned off the main street to head north, the road leading up to home had been bricked in and painted, of all things, a bright yellow. It was a yellow-brick road!

"How great!" Drew was impressed. "How can anybody miss us now?"

There at the top and to the right stood Llangolen West, home to twenty-four talented people. They had been busy with their dream.

Drew's hair, blonde and curly, bobbed in the sunlight as she dropped her long legs to the side of the drive.

"Hey, my home!"

Each unit had been painted white in the two months she had been gone, and with new board and batten applied, a contrast. The entire compound had been landscaped just before her arrival. Up under the trees new grass was springing up in the benchmarks left over from festival time.

To Drew, the agony of the past had dimmed; here at her work

place she would find the minds she needed to complete her plans.

CHAPTER ELEVEN

Setting the Stage

The town pleased Drew more than ever. It sparkled with new activity. She took her car around the bend to the north where the sea cattle grazed on the high grassy slopes. The road paralleled the Brigadoon shores, laced with creamy surf.

Here in this town there was the flavor of Northern California before it ever became *California.* The inland arroyo carried them a little distance from driving winter storms. These storms were a month away, late November or December.

On the main street that morning, Drew ran into Carolyn, who was walking into the dusty interior of the village's Italian grocery. Huge salamis hung from the ceiling, along with twisted cheeses, and an excellent collection of California chardonnay and Madeira wines lined the shelves.

Carolyn laid down her bag of bread and waited for Drew to buy salami and Italian olives.

"What's up with you?"

Drew answered her quietly, "Could you stop by the apartment? I've got a need to do something at the bank."

A gleam of interest came into Carolyn's eye, but she couldn't ask too many questions, not here in the market. Too many ears. The townspeople would pick up the waves of a business deal. Already many people of the town were sullenly suspicious of so many women congregating at the white cottages above the bakery. All this energy and hustle-bustle was good for business, but the locals were hostile.

Drew added a few words to get Carolyn informed. "I've got to do something about the formation of a true school, to get accredited. We need a new loan in order to make a larger place for the conservatory."

"You have a lot more people staying there?"

Carolyn knew that Drew had a good background in music theory, having attended a fine university in the southland. She had a Master's Degree and had gone on toward a Doctorate. She looked at Drew inquiringly.

"Yes, wouldn't you probably have met them? There are two women here from Julliard. Didn't you meet that one from Toronto?"

"Can't remember. Where are you putting them? Is there any room?"

"They're bunched together into the cubicles above the main shed, the dining room... in the dormitory." Carolyn wasn't sure about the classes, nor who was teaching them. Her work had been in English literature. She had met Drew while at USC, but they had been in different fields. Even at that time, however, there had been a charisma about Drew that attracted many people to her. Drew had married, right from graduation, sometime in her early twenties, but the marriage had lasted just a few years.

"Is anybody in the units selling out?" Carolyn wanted to know.

"No, they're all working out pretty well. Actually, for me, I'm getting stronger, leaving that old life behind. I've been laying these new plans. Also, I've been running every day. I can run six miles now, not every day, of course."

"Do you have a running partner?"

"We don't run alone, we've got three women who run together, up the big road leading to Park Hill, through those trees," Drew pointed her hand toward the south.

"When do you want to talk about a new addition?" Carolyn in her businesslike way always returned to the point.

"Dinner tonight?"

"Fine," said Carolyn. "What time shall I come?"

"About seven. Come to the compound."

Drew carried her groceries to the van, thinking how happy she was to be set back on the track again. How good it felt to be out of the hospital! She planted her foot firmly on the accelerator, intending to take a drive by herself. Her brown-gold hair was dulled in the sunshine, but her skin and eyes were clear. The running technique was paying off.

Feeling carefree and unprogrammed, she bypassed the turn to the brick road and headed up the flat grassland highway on the way to Hearst Castle. Right at the turn, the narrow curving roadbed dipped into tortuous mountain embankments where hundreds of feet below, long breakers ran up the sands. She was looking for an isolated beach to eat her salami and bread. The beach for the Hearst area was too populated, so she continued up the highway where a rock slide had closed the wild section up to Monterey. Now the debris had finally been cleared. She drove on.

At Lucia, the tiny brick wooden station was closed. It overhung one of the most beautiful bays in the world. Right at the top of a cornice reminiscent of Riviera sea cliffs, the rustic buildings were overgrown with a Kudzu vine which engulfed even the telephone lines. All was quiet and deserted. The ocean glistened in a steel-colored sheet to the south promontory that was Llangolen. The white trim on the red wooden store was a good contrast to the blue ocean beyond.

Drew pulled up to a road-building pile of black tar and got out. This place was a meeting ground for huge drug exchanges. She had been aware of this, but no people were in sight at this time. Nobody was in the store. She wished she could be sharing this seacoast with someone. It would be nice to share her lunch too. On the other hand, she thought about the limitation in a new way. At least she didn't have anyone bothering her. She wasn't wasting her life in nightly partying. She wasn't high, and she could think about how things were going in Llangolen.

What professors? What kind of music? Should it be only serious music? She thought it definitely should be experimental in design. They had people arriving with all manner of backgrounds, classical guitars, as well as rock musicians. They needed a new voice... something different in the music. Even now she felt an aura of excitement about the place that everybody was feeling, a youthful energy as newcomers from all the states arrived. She had to shape it, had to be the force. She wanted the best for Llangolen, even though she missed a certain companionship.

The sea and sky soothed her uncertain mood, and she drove back into Llangolen ready to go to work.

After six weeks had elapsed from the time in the clinic, Drew was looking at home and Llangolen with fresh eyes. She was completely away from the substance abuse and was again taking up her leadership duties. She was as sparkling as the coast which showed itself a cerulean blue from Carmel to Guadalupe. Promise was in the air.

"Let's see, Jean." Drew was quizzing her. "This Bearcat Bookstore has been going for two months; have we any profit yet?"

"Between the innkeepers and Michelle and Gretyl, we are operating, not in the black yet, just investing in book stock, but the accounting procedure is set up; it is a viable business," Jean had some words that were optimistic. "Of course, we're losing money at first."

"I hope I can pull the strings together for the school part of it. I need to be responsible for all this, not a patient who drags down the rest," Drew's tone was apologetic.

"Yes. And we need you. We don't have a target goal any more, now the summer festival is over. You need to get back where you're headed."

"Yeah, I think I'm back physically; now I'll take time to think and focus. Shouldn't take too long."

A new woman had come to the compound one week before Drew returned from the hospital. She had moved into the square bungalow which had two doors. The second half had six tatami Japanese mats in the cubicle. Her unit had an extended sun porch to the south side, and it was from her own sunporch that Jean observed this new woman, resting in her jogging shorts and red headband. Whoever she was, she appeared to be a serious runner. Every day, seven until nine in the morning, she ran down the hill into the main street of town, over the highway which was the link to the coast, into the long curve of hill that held pines and the cottages of the older section of the coastal arroyo. She seemed to be doing a half-marathon, perhaps six or seven miles. A good portion of her day was spent in running.

Two days after returning, Drew was standing with one foot on her van door jam, when the new woman approached. She was slender, not as tall as Drew, but her body was slight and long-waisted. Her long brown hair was tied into a ponytail. She walked up to Drew, graceful and slim now, her heavier running clothes pared down to a summer festival tank top and shorts. Drew could feel a heightening of interest as the girl approached. She noticed how her hazel eyes had gold glints.

"You're the new arrival to the compound?" Drew hesitated before getting into the front seat of her van.

The woman looked at her, her face preoccupied with a sort of question as though she wasn't sure what she wanted from her. Drew could feel her own face redden under the close scrutiny.

Karen broke off in a confusion, "Oh, I'm looking to see when the bookstore will open."

Drew, not looking away, mumbled, "Oh, somewhere about twelve. Things don't get started around here till about noon . . ."

She could see how disappointed Karen was. "But I just wanted to check a source for myself. It's about a press address."

Drew put her feet back on the drive. "Maybe I could help you. I have a key for the downstairs. I think they're out of town, anyway."

The younger woman flushed, "If you could let me in for five minutes, I wouldn't disturb anything else. I know where that listing is."

Drew hesitated and then suggested, "Come on in with me."

"You seem to know your way around here." There was a knowing little smile on her lips. Drew judged the young woman to be in her early thirties. Karen seemed at ease with her supple body, and Drew felt tall and awkward suddenly beside her. As they walked in toward the desk, she deliberately recovered her rightful sense of authority. She looked the woman in the eye.

"They'll have a fit if they find out I was in here." Karen smiled as if they were in on a secret.

"I'll tell them what happened. It's okay. After all, I own the upstairs." Drew didn't really care about such a breach in property rights, and she felt a sudden jump of interest in this girl.

"Just write your name on this check-out slip, so they'll know who's made off with things."

Karen B. McAllister, printed the young woman, bending low over the counter. Her breasts were small, firm, indented under the tank top as she leaned on the counter. Drew felt a rush of admiration for the way she had kept discipline with her running. She measured mentally the length of Karen's back, which was similar to her own, but smaller.

"And address?"

"It's Llangolen. I've just moved in the other half of the end cottage."

"Oh, you're living here? With that piano player?"

"Just the other half of her place. Kinda roommates in that duplex."

"Oh," Drew let the woman get halfway out the door before she thought, "What about the I.D., some sort of identification if you take that pamphlet away, so they can find you again?"

The girl hesitated, confused. "Here, I've got this gold bracelet. It's got my name on it."

"Then I'll know you'll return it," Drew grinned at her.

"You seem to be sort of in charge around here," the girl seemed reluctant to end the conversation between them.

"Yes, well, I'm one of the original founders. Now floundering," she chuckled, thinking of the unformed chaos ahead of her. "Say, you seem to be doing some jogging. I wish I could say the same."

"Why don't you start a little?"

"I've run a little. I used to jump on the trampoline a lot."

"Well, then, your legs are probably good. Here now, I can't bother you any longer."

But Drew felt the lingering glance of sexual interest make her face heat. She knew the exchange had gone on as long as decent propriety would allow, and neither of them knew what to say next. So Drew wheeled on her foot back to her truck. She took the I.D. bracelet out and placed it into the little box on the dashboard.

She felt the eyes of the woman still on her as she slipped the car into reverse, pushed the vehicle back onto the entry drive and wheeled around to go into town. As she drove away from the compound, she could see the woman staring after her truck until she rounded their corner down into town.

CHAPTER TWELVE

Meeting Time

The bright blue days of October stretched on, each like the other, until at last the unbroken sunshine abruptly ended as they came to the eve of the meeting weekend. The night before the people were to arrive, a strange heaviness came over them, a sadness, and around nine o'clock as people were arriving, a flickering wind gusted up, died, and then blew in earnest, bending the tops of trees, rustling the few palms and pampas grass. A weather change, a lonely prelude to those hard-driving winter storms along the coast. The sea, normally bright green, turned ugly, muddy gray, and huge rolling breakers came in on the bathing cove. All night the wind whipped the bushes against the nestled English cottages, and again the next morning, the stiff breeze continued, this time bringing sprinkled rain that discolored the outside cement driveway. People hurried into the small auditorium after tossing bedrolls into the dormitory. It was to be an indoor weekend.

A newness came forth into the courtyard and into the central dining hall that had not been there before. Energy was being supplied from many women in their thirties; most came from northern California. Drew talked to one woman who had been born in Arizona or New Mexico, but had gone to Toronto to study music. She had long flowing fuzzy hair and the face, not beautiful, had eyes glassy with intelligence.

Capable, that's the only way to describe it, thought Drew as she turned to face the entire group from the platform. The girl sat in the front row in red faded levis; she had nubile shoulders in her muscle sweat top.

A few couples scattered around the auditorium—many single women, some men musicians of all varieties, members of groups from Oakland and Mendocino. All the women went into the conference. Drew led them confidently, leaving a clear plan of action, parliamentarily correct. As soon as she felt a digression, she gently reminded them, led them into committees, suggested times and how to get the advertising and donations they needed.

The next general target date for recital and concert after the summer had passed was to be sometime in late April. They hammered out their leadership positions in a matter-of-fact manner that would have made the Board of General Petroleum gasp. Soon Sunday night came, and they had to return to numerous cities. Drew, Jane, and Karen watched the ragged Volkswagons drive off into the clearing Sunday evening. Long purple clouds paralleled the line of the serene ocean.

Drew had questioned her own mind before the meeting; would her mental powers be diminished because of her previous illness? Was she still capable? Could she remember things? But this conference had only restored her confidence. Everyone accepted her leadership without question.

Drew heaved a sigh of contentment. She thought, it went off without playing hell with my nerves. I didn't have a drink and look how steady my hands are.

Jean looked at her. Drew seemed up in spirits, but not in an excitement state, rather filled with quiet confidence. Jean knew that she was happy about the Toronto woman who had decided to stay on.

"About twelve of these people are still here, and they aren't going home for at least a week."

She pondered, "Well, if we feed them, we could build on an addition or set a floor for the conservatory."

And so the next week was a jumble of getting to know the women who intended to stay, planning and staking out the new music floor which stretched in three tiers up the pine woods across the long shed dining hall.

At night, impromptu music was played, guitars were taken up after they had all gathered for beef bourguignon, artichoke and lettuce salad, and rustic Danish loaves from the Danish bakery on the street below them. Drew found herself at dinner talking to Karen, the new woman in the muscle shirt.

"You're out here just for a vacation?"

"Well, I've had a teaching post for a half year, but it was a temporary fill-in for a sabbatical leave in the valley. Now I'm looking for another half-year or year's post."

"Have you gotten your credentials recently?"

"Yes, two years ago in Toronto."

"You could put in your resume in San Luis or Santa Maria and wait it out here."

"Thanks, I would like that situation. Some California seacoast as a change from Toronto sounds good to me."

Through the next weeks, Drew contacted some friends in the nearby colleges. They spread the word about Karen's need for a short-term contract, for six months or so. Since her credits were impeccable, they had no anxiety about finding something to support her allowing her to stay for awhile in Llangolen. As it turned out, there was a sudden illness in the Economics Department at a nearby college, and Drew's friends put forward Karen's name. By January she was notified she had a job until June and perhaps for one additional semester. It all fit in. Karen signed the contract and continued to live at Llangolen. So Karen was added to the crowd of regulars.

Gradually feeling the need for some fun after all the hard work of the summer, Drew, Jean, and Karen decided to get on the sea. Drew knew how to sail and, in the harbor town, she found a good buy on a twenty-five foot boat with roughed-up paint which was definitely seaworthy. In the mornings, they worked to lay out wooden forms for the cement base of the conservatory. From two-thirty on, they played.

Several weekends were spent at the end of the marina, taking six people aboard, plying up and down the long passageway of water which led past the sandspit to the open water. With three aboard who knew how to sail, Drew and Jean had plenty of help with the lines, and they experimented with drafts of winds which came up suddenly. They didn't ever leave the breakwater entrance to deep water.

Karen was a fine addition, even if she was from a land-locked state. Her long-boned frame seemed to cling to the boards of the boat; the bottoms of her bare feet were high-arched and agile. She never got cold, and soon Drew had her handle the tiller with Jean in the middle and herself at the spinnaker.

"Let's go wing-and-wing back to the marina."

Stretching both mainsails out to left and right as Drew suggested, they picked up enough breeze to fly down past all the harbor restaurants, down where brown pelicans roosted on the pilings. The sky was still a bright blue in this November weather, but one mid-week storm had shattered their halcyon fall days, peppering Llangolen with a cold rain and drenching the inside of their sailboat. Still, the weekends held good, and they continued to spend their afternoons out in the clear air. One day, only Drew, Jean, and Karen were aboard, bailing and sponging out their hull, draining the petcock. Jean watched the two of them together; the bond was growing stronger. Drew and Karen often practiced together. They were also planning out a course of study for this school which had been shaped up in Toronto.

"Not many of these weekends left, and we'd better watch out for winter storms." Jean looked at the whitening sky.

"That's right. Not much time left. I wonder if we could manage the boat alone, Karen. Jean is going down to L.A. the next two weekends. Do we dare handle it, you on the front sail?"

"I'm fairly sure of myself now."

They both looked out to the purple line of the sea which made a gap at the end of the channel. In the water otters were playing on their backs as Drew's craft soundlessly passed, out beside the great rock which gave name to the harbor home.

"Look at those pelicans diving for sardines!"

"Hold on, here is the opening. Look how the color changes!"

"Kid, that's not too scary; it's only water."

The entranceway to the harbor was breached, Jean a little apprehensive as the sea beyond came up in long curls against the chunky talus rimming the huge rock above them. Spouting spray came over the man-made breakwater. Reluctantly Drew turned the boat around; she wanted to be in the real sea, if only for a mile or two toward the small fishing village to the north. Karen was a good foil for her; she had some daring and flamboyance that was also part of Drew. They wanted to go on, but Jean demurred, cutting short the trip. She had work to do at home.

"All right, but I really want to get out in the open sea a little bit. Don't you, Karen?"

"Yes, I'll go with you next time, and we'll make it out of the calm harbor." They looked at each other in agreement.

They returned through the channel and anchored the boat at the end of the long marina.

Three more days and evenings passed with hectic activity, the floorings on the hillside alive with wheelbarrows, hired hands, equipment, the volunteers from the town, and inhabitants of Llangolen.

The studings were set in place, and the cement pouring was ready to begin. Huge trucks came up from the outskirts of the next town, and Drew helped the contractor who was in charge of the setting of cement. Finally, the finishers came and trowelled it smooth. The rest of them all watched. Twelve men completed all in a short time, but the volunteers were helping hauling and carrying.

Drew was present at all the operations, in a hopeful state of mind as she supervised and answered questions. This was to be a new kind of conservatory. How she had chafed under the educational hand vise which had gripped her and many others! There was something about the indoctrinization of the system which made it hard to be creative, to be oneself.

For instance, certain scores of music were to be used for young people. The college students were clamped into those composers which were "acceptable." When these graduates went out into the teaching world, the principals of their schools were the overseers of what performances were "acceptable." And so on. It gagged her to think about such accepted rules. The artist was squeezed into the same mold, practitioners of what was taught in their graduate schools. The literature teacher was instructed how to take apart Joseph Conrad's *Heart of Darkness* for preparation to teach sixteen- and seventeen-year-olds. In this way, thousands of graduates poured out the same material all over again. Everyone was subjected to the same thing. And *if* you wanted a job in the system, you had to comply. Thus the bodies of knowledge became watered into a gruel as bland as Cream of Wheat. And the artist, (musician), was squeezed out. The artist was not respected. Nowhere in the country was there enough money to support live creativity. Small string groups of musicians were not subsidized; they merely got together to play on their own. The Cream of

Wheat (farming industry) had been subsidized in America, but not the cream of its youth. Drew thought to herself, if we are not careful, we'll become the pablum of which administration and ruling managers are made. And some fierce energy-filled people will take us over. Some country we don't know of yet, that allows new thought to spring up.

So Drew thought; the truly vibrant and intelligent young are forced out of each profession, disgusted, while the dutiful keep at it. How glad she was to be able to start over. The music that was taught at Llangolen would not be altogether classical; classical was technique; there was to be a rock element merged, intertwined. There were no rules; this was an experimental school. No rules.

Drew's thought drifted back in time as she watched her friends and the hired laborers finishing the cement flooring.

There had been a man in her life *once*. She took a flashback to the time in her senior year when they had lived together, along with the following year when they both taught in the L.A. basin as part of that huge school system. Since then, there had been a number of relationships, though mostly with women. Drew's thoughts skipped around vaguely, springing from girl to girl; only a few of these pictures were still crisp in her mind as she skimmed over the endless round of parties, the late nights which added up and now summarized ten years. There was no need for achievement, just a seeking of pleasure. She took her gang to each party, then hauled them off to some bar at two o'clock. She saw that this had led to several physical breakdowns. Hard lifestyle was not good for heart and body; there was that time, too, she had run a high fever for three weeks in the hospital.

Now that something new was possible, this new idea on which she based her existence, there was no longer any need to wear herself out. This was a new feeling, a strength of nerve. She could feel that freshness. Thus, she reflected, the reason for her move into Llangolen was becoming a reality, and she could see in perspective how the administrative straight jacket had been leading to her downfall.

She felt free. And she wanted to play.

Everyone around her was bending to the end goal now, sensitive in hand and mind; nevertheless, they were out pouring cement, hoeing sand, and pounding boards.

The brightness of the air, as well as the dropping off of disillusion, made Drew feel like a fourteen-year-old. It was a dream shaping up, shaping her up, moving her into a creative reality.

Now the hillside brigade was standing around the edge of the slope. They half slipped down into the forms. All her friends, plus the new people cleaned up the boards, picked up the tools, balanced on their toes as they watched the finishers. By Friday at twelve, the job was completed. The hired workmen laid down their tools and went home for the weekend, letting the cement dry on its own. Drew knelt down and initialed the cement. Everyone around sent up a cry of accomplishment. There it was, forever. They stood in amazement that they had been able to build, these professional musicians. For once they quelled their independent egos and bound themselves to a larger task. They couldn't believe their "heroine" strength.

"Let's go for a sail. We're all done here. It's our reward." Drew was already riding the wave. Now her joy was spilling over. She laughed. She shouted.

She could envision the practice rooms rising up from the flooring and new studs. It was happening in front of her, even despite illness and all other obstacles. The reality of the school was as solid as the concrete in carefully graded tiers. Why not have a small escape to the sea? Down to the sea in ships, she thought. She glanced Karen's way.

Since her episode with spinal meningitis, Drew had seemed one-dimensional to her friends, careless, perhaps even callous in her relationships with her friends. One after another, they had felt scorned by her, as she ran her own life with someone new. She had not meant to. Her attention wafted to new sports and enthusiasms.

Now she was continuing, Jean observed. Since Jean was unable to go sailing, only the two of them would go. Jean was headed for L.A. that morning for an interview with a young pianist. The girl was a budding virtuoso of eleven. She had to get to this girl by five o'clock. One by one, the others pleaded tiredness, but Karen's eyebrows went up, alert to being alone with Drew.

Drew felt a great glee in having a chance to get away with Karen. Before this time, they had felt a need to have a buffer between them, a smoke screen to hide their mounting interest in each other.

Drew felt her heart jump as Karen said, "Yes, I'll go with you. Let's start before the afternoon is gone."

The sky was a strong blue as they headed south in Drew's van, the weather almost hot. Too hot for November; it was strange, thought Drew. By the time they had driven four miles to the marina, a low string of gray clouds had crept up out at sea. They cast off the tarp on the boat and let loose the lines.

"We'll go out anyway," said Drew, casting an eye at the sky which had a forboding look. No November storms had appeared.

"It's a hot day," but Karen pulled on extra sweat pants. "Do you think I'll need a windbreaker?"

"Yep, I'd take it. I want to clear the rock this time, and it's sure to be cold. We haven't been outside the breakwater yet, but..."

"Can you and I manage this alone?"

"If you know how to fix the lines when we come about..."

"Of course." Karen had sailed before.

It was decided.

"Let's go past the rock about a mile. Then we'll get close into shore and make our turn." Drew wasn't ready to go out into the ocean.

"Okay, I'm ready," Karen settled herself flat on the deck, and the light boat took off smoothly into the breeze. They sailed past small craft by the Harbor Hut and up the straight channel to the sea. They spent half an hour passing some fishermen on the banks. In that time they could see more clouds building on the low horizon.

"Let's chance it anyway. The part I want to sail could take an hour up north and half an hour fast sailing coming in." Drew had made her decision.

Karen got up front and stretched out on the foredeck. "It's hot, but toss me my windbreaker for the sail past the rock."

"Better put it on now. Here we go," Drew had the rudder. Already the wind was chilly, and the water spraying into their faces was cold.

They sailed out the breakwater and into long, low swells. The wind picked up, and they found themselves racing, flying to the northern part of the rock. This was an entirely different ride, compared to the calm inlet they had left ten minutes before.

Waves had began to slap at them, larger and more foam-tipped. Drew strained at the rudder. She had planned to go forward, so she braced her back against the tiller. She leaned heavily when a wave struck broadside.

In five minutes the sun was obscured. Instead of a light scudding, they were out in a strong sea. Drew didn't know now whether to turn back or steer horizontally. She didn't have the expertise for this. They were directly seaward now, about five hundred yards from the rock's talus, scree rock, and cement breakwater. Drew looked out to sea. She barely had time to glimpse an impossibly high wave which covered the horizon. A moment of comprehension; then all senses stiffened; she had a loss of feeling.

"This can't be. It just doesn't look right. This can't be happening." Drew had time only for that flash of thought.

With one long swell to preview, the wave (what they call a 'rogue' wave) bore down on them, cracking and curling, picking up the sailboat with Drew and Karen, lifting them entirely above the huge pile of breakwater rocks. They were all dashed together. Somehow, Drew was holding the tiller. Karen was somewhere at the front, clinging to the mast, but down, down on the land as the water sucked about them. Drew and Karen were crumpled together with stray boards as the wall of water spent itself on the roadway, climbing half-way up on the rock. Each grabbed a handhold on a rock and clung as if they were ticks on skin, but this time to a board. Ribs bumped against rocks, shoulders were scraped by cruel iron pieces, knees cracked. They couldn't feel their injuries, but somehow they hung on as the water gurgled and swirled backward. Sand and boards and mast of the sailboat, junk now, filtered back seaward.

Still, they were alive, clinging to their rocks. As water receded, they looked for place holds to pull up high on the big rock. They wanted to get sixty feet in the air, thinking how to get to safety, but weren't quick enough.

Drew's terrible eyesight was limited to two feet in front of her, and her vision was still blurry. She was pulling her way upward and over rocks to face the huge morro. She was bruised and her clothing torn; blood was streaming into her eyes. She wasn't looking seaward, but toward the land.

"Drew, look out!" Karen shrieked.

Karen turned back in horror. While they were trying to rescue themselves from the first onslaught, a second wave was approaching, curling white and muddy at the bottom.

"Grab something, anything," she spat it out fast. Drew lashed a hand out at a projecting corrugated metal sheet which had a rusty cable attached and placed her body in the V angle.

The second mountainous wave hit; carrying Karen further inland, but Drew was inundated and, for an endless time, held her breath as the water covered her; then the deep water relinquished its hold and drizzled back seaward. She had kept her handhold.

The wave made its last cracking impact on the land.

Drew was scraped along her rib cage and underarm. Her forehead was bleeding, red running lines. She had one deck shoe left, the other foot was slashed along the instep. Slowly she grappled her way over some higher rocks, painfully sliding her feet and legs into leg-breaking places, able at last to crawl onto the high land and roadway. A few cars were parked there.

Karen caught sight of her, dully comprehending that they were both alive. They looked at each other in horror. Drew looked dull and bloodied, ill-kempt. She looked like driftwood. They eased themselves onto a sandy shale that made up part of the roadway. There was a car, but nobody was in it. It was plain that they had to walk back to find help.

Both women picked their way down the road, blood bathing Drew's face, Karen with scarcely any clothes. Neither had shoes. A man and wife walking toward them glanced their way, then looked down. They didn't want to see, rejected what they saw.

They were like displaced refugees.

"Please, can't you help?" asked Karen.

The couple continued toward their car, got in and drove away.

The two women scuffed and limped inland on the gravel at dead level with the side of the rock. Some small boys looked at them curiously, then pointed and jeered, "Look at her boobs. She hasn't any clothes on."

They were nearly naked except for some pants and torn tee

shirts, Karen without her windbreaker. Farther along the flint-like roadbed, they met another rebuff; one slanting glance of disapproval, then embarrassed, a fisherman dodged behind his truck. They shambled on for the better part of an hour, until Karen spotted the gray cottage of the official coast guard rescue building. They fell into the doorway. Two men were working the desk. They grasped the problem, having rescued people at sea before. This wasn't the first accident at the rock. By law, people were forbidden to climb the rock because of dangers involved.

When they saw how broken these women were, they sprang into action. An ambulance came within fifteen minutes and drove them twenty miles into the emergency entrance of an excellent hospital. They were carefully put on pallets and examined for their injuries. They were lucky to be alive.

"I can't believe it. Nobody would help us!" Drew gasped out to one of the attendants.

"Yeah, not your usual Good Samaritan Story," said Karen with a sigh.

Both women were put into one double hospital room. After several phone calls to Llangolen and a general inspection and washing of their wounds, each was placed in a separate room to have her wounds tended. Drew drifted off to sleep with a dim vision of the prophesy about the rock in her mind.

At the identical time of the boat accident, Jean drove alone down Highway 101, passing the green hills of Lompoc and Buelton. She had plenty of time to think. For an anxious five minutes, she worried about her two friends sailing out on the Pacific Bay, but she dismissed the thought, reflecting that they had been out in the craft five or six times before. She conceded that she might as well pursue something else.

She thought herself back in time, remembering how life had changed since she had been locked into the old job. For five or six years, she had felt the need to cut a low profile, thus escaping detection as a non-submissive person. The rationalization behind this lay in a stubborn fear that male administrators could make her post uncomfortable, perhaps reduce her salary or cut her duties to routine. We have to live to fight again, she thought, or was it fight to live? Either way, nobody could control her mind if she kept quiet and did her work the conventional way: none would know her secret, her revolutionary nature. Her basic view was that most women resorted to this. She knew that confidences to other women were made carefully away from the ears of men. If men only knew it was twice as bad as they could guess. Her real views were not posted on her office door. The office door was clean. Safe. No advertisement of the heat she felt.

Now she had more freedom, but deep feelings of loneliness remained. Even though she was housed in an enclave of feminists, she still needed someone for herself. If only there would be some counterpart, artistic or literary, someone closer to her age. Why was she always planning activities with someone twenty years her junior? The habit was bound to lead to disaster; she would be alone. This wisdom lay muted most of the time, but the natural attraction had remained through her forties and fifties. A May-December worry hung about her like a cawl. People would mention it occasionally, and she herself thought it odd from time to time.

When she remembered this, she thought, well we just learn from one another. At times, though, the wind would howl outside her south sun porch, and she would become almost hysterical. Those were just the mean times.

Now with Drew, she had a friendship that was non-communicative. She couldn't voice such misgivings to Drew. "Oh, get off it. Just smoke a joint and it'll be all right!" was Drew's usual response to inner jitters. Drew's personality was closer to that of a twenty-year-old boy out to do a daredevil dog fight in World War I, Jean thought. She wished on the one hand, she could be more like Drew and, on the other, she wished for someone, a timeless friend to hold long talks with, perhaps sitting on a veranda.

Yes, that's it, she thought as she slipped into fantasy and almost drove off the road. I wish I could sit on a broad veranda, a low-railed porch with overhang and shadowy rooms inside, where literary or artistic friends would come for nourishing weekends.

Yet, something was missing. That faceless companion behind the veranda. Somebody would turn up to enchain her interest, someone always had before, someone with convoluted personality quirks. Jean determined to go look at some real estate along the east road of town as soon as she returned. When I plan a change, my circumstances change. It always happens, she thought with comfort.

The L.A. freeways then took her attention, and she reminded herself to turn off on the San Diego freeway and not be led into the central part of L.A.

CHAPTER THIRTEEN

The Conservatory

Jean returned from a successful interview with a child prodigy, an eleven-year-old girl from an Eastern state. The girl was there in L.A., along with the mother, a Mrs. Jacobson, and a very different man, David McClintock, who was a dynamic promoter of the child. They were not related. When she got back from her trip, she located Drew and Karen in the hospital.

They had remained for treatment in separate rooms, Drew being nursed for a broken femur and a severe head wound, plus interior wrenching. Karen had to have a broken collar bone set, was put in a cast, had broken her wrist and had the rib cage taped. Wounds from the scrapes on their sides and backs had to be bandaged every day. Their hospital stay began in November, and the ordeal wasn't over until March 15. What started out as a breezy sailing trip became a five-month recovery.

They told Jean all the details of the accident, and Jean, in turn, gave them news of a possible notable addition to their school. After some negotiation with hospital authorities, they devised a scheme to have one large hospital room with two beds; this helped the three of them to talk about their plans together. This way, they got a lot of nurturing from nurses and from one another. Drew longed for the day when she could stretch out in the sun deck behind her upper apartment at Llangolen. How to enlarge this? Karen also needed a lot of sun. Build an addition just to accommodate a friend? In the meantime, they had plenty of time to talk. They were recouping their strength. At first, they couldn't stay awake for three hours.

Jean felt saddled with the management of the new conservatory. The plans had all been laid for the raising of roofs and practice rooms in the big building under the pines. All the loan money had been established in the bank and the workmen hired. So they just went ahead as scheduled.

The building obviously had to go on. So Jean supervised. Twelve small practice rooms were joisted and the siding started. The large auditorium and the green receiving room on the basement floor were completed by the workmen in January and February. Everytime a new decision had to be made, Jean went into the hospital to converse with the other two. They were now able to remain awake for half a day, and their wounds were not so severe. They had no strength, but their minds were alive. More than the physical recovery, they were together in wanting the same goal. They were caught up in an innovative West Coast Music School.

The formulation of the building was not all. The making of a curriculum and accreditation letters had to be filled out, and encounters with artistic members of the school had to be worked out. Jean felt blocked, as Drew was physically blocked, until they simply worked out a system of "Yes" or "No" at the hospital that enabled them to move forward. Jean got secretarial help from Gretyl, and then she reported daily to the hospital. There was so much running around to do. She knew that she shelved her private longings for a partner to share things. She was too busy. She told herself her days were full.

Most of the time she brought natural fruit and vegetables from the town. The news of the planning committee for the second Festival in April had to be shared. This constant contact among the three of them allowed Drew her input as the chief leader of the triumvirate, while Jean did the actual management.

Along with the framing of the conservatory, there was the complication of the negotiation between herself and David McClintock. This dealt with the adding on of the child piano player, Aurora Jacobson. He was a strange man, not really sexually compelling, but intelligent-looking, and possessing so much energy that Jean was happy in his company. He not only was interested in getting Aurora established, but he knew authors, and he was in touch with New York and L.A. happenings. That was important. Jean met him in Santa Maria where Mrs. Jacobson was, and also she went to small theater with him in L.A. Through David, Jean found herself meeting other people in the music and theater world of the Southland. She wondered at his constant presence in the compound, but he took her mind off her solitary state and projected her into a larger world.

David was loud, irreverent and irritating. Sometimes he sent her chasing off on impossible errands, but he would look at her with his wide blue eyes, and he seemed so childishly sincere that she would comply. He was around five feet ten, not handsome, but presentable. He did forge this contact between the small girl who was soon to be famous and this new talked-about music school in the West.

Thus, the frequent visitors, the laughing and general high spirits made Karen and Drew's hospital room a place of celebration, rather than a melancholy obligation. The long months of recuperation, their mutual suffering, their hopes toward a future in Llangolen brought them closer together. They could plan a year ahead together. Drew was happy even though she knew Karen might someday return to her native Toronto. When they were driven home in March in Drew's van, they got out still limping and broken, but they were a couple.

Karen moved slowly, watching the long step from the van to the driveway. Drew moved in a crab-like motion out the sliding doors. Her broken leg and twisted arm had not mended straight, but she would be able to play instruments. Their bodies were stiff from lack of exercise.

But a cheer greeted their awkward movements. Around thirty people had gathered for their homecoming, even David McClintock was among them; Jean was glad to see his loyalty. She stood at the Bearcat Bookstore, greeting them, along with the entire staff. The selling of books had been brisk; their accounts had been almost in the black, and in the front room many poetry readings had taken place.

All the staff had gleefully strung the low-ceilinged room with bunches of balloons. Sixteen bottles of Moet champagne rested in ice, black caviar was embedded in shredded egg, and on the center table rested a resplendent frosted pink walnut cake.

They were so happy! "Look what we have! We've been waiting for this day. Take Karen up to the loft to see how we have the bedroom fixed."

Drew made the slow assent, taking Karen with her good arm pressed behind her. Somehow it was better to leave all the rest downstairs with their celebrating. Good to be within their circle of friends, but she was grateful to get Karen alone. Content with each other now they were alone, they looked at the checkered sewn quilt hanging over the high basket chair; a fluffy down comforter blue with blue cornflowers covered their bed, and through the open window a small box of geraniums nodded. Soft breezes came across the top of the arroyo that housed the main street of Llangolen. March was upon them, the spring was approaching, and they were at home in time.

The conservatory was almost completed.

"Hey, you wanta stay up there for awhile? Rest up?" yelled Jean.

Drew looked at Karen strangely. She yelled back down the stairs. "Mind? We're tired after the ride. We'll be down after a little nap."

Looking at Jean's retreating back, Drew cupped a hand around Karen's shoulder.

"Come on, we haven't kissed each other since that hospital room."

"I know, it was always full of nurses," murmured Karen. Slowly Drew placed her arm and hand around Karen's waist, taking time to remove her cotton shirt, drawing her carefully down into the bed nook.

"Can't you, can't they?"

"Of course, but they won't ever come up here."

Drew found the down coverlet and laid Karen under it, leaving one corner open to the stiffening breeze from the window. Then she quickly limped in beside her, on top of her, expertly placing her body where each limb exactly covered the other, smothering her, pushing her into the surface of the mattress. It was a total immersion and fusion, awaited for months in that hospital room. She had visualized it for months. She felt Karen relax in absolute submission.

The thing was done so expertly, thought Karen in grateful surrender. "I've wanted this for so long."

Soon they lost consciousness of what was going on below them in the bookstore. Drew felt Karen rise to her in a long, shuddering spasm and then they both fell asleep for a two hour rest.

The rock rose up in a crazy dream, seeming to bring forth Drew's aunt's prophesy. I'll get something back from this, she thought sleepily as she came to. "I survived the rock; now what was that about a monster?" Roofs reared up in her dream, pianos, standards. Eccentric and white-haired teachers. Classes, being late for class. Dim plans faded as Drew really slept.

CHAPTER FOURTEEN

Morning Star Rising

Two days later Drew walked around the completed conservatory while looking over the blueprints. The terraced sections were enclosed now. Only a small limp advertised her accident, although she was still stiff in the long femur incision they had operated on. She was a thirty-nine-year-old Directress, and she was beautiful. Wherever she went, people stared at her, sneaked small glances to see and confirm, yes, different, beautiful.

They had lost a few of the cypress trees because of the two side annexes, but the entire new addition was ringed with green; some lawn was left by the roadway. The rough cut redwood exterior blended in well under the pines.

"Drew, darn, I'm having the hardest time getting five minutes with you. I want to talk about some things," Jean complained as they walked through the entrance. "Look, it's done now, twelve practice rooms. They are small, but look how they're fitted out! The money just came floating in while you were gone. Thousands of endowments. And three rich widows gave a substantial sum. Two people from Santa Barbara shelled out money. Two grants were even sewed up from the government. We had money from many sources. Carolyn took care of all the banking and accounting. You know her, all business."

"Bet you thought you saw the last of me floating out," Drew remarked wryly, referring to her accident. "Not much help to you then, was I?" Drew was best on a light note. Jean had found they communicated only on ordinary practical things; it had been that way for months now, and nothing about Karen was said. She was, she admitted, a bit jealous, but that was because she didn't have anybody.

"Look now at the auditorium. It can seat 135 people," Jean continued. "It's just about ready, and our classes will start for spring April 15, going to mid-June. There will be a summer session ending in August." Jean was excited at how much the school had grown physically. "You should see the people floating around.

There's money in the crowd coming here."

"What's happening for teaching, composers? Which reminds me, is that old Steiglitz from Santa Barbara here?"

"Yes, he's moved into town, up on the hill. Also, a well-known pianist from Hollywood is located on Parkhurst Hill. People in theater, directors, actors have changed from the Santa Barbara area. They seem to have money to spend, and they are spending it. We have two people—from Scripps or Pomona, I've forgotten which—slated to teach harmony." Jean went on about the scheduling.

"Anyhow, you're trying to tell me the place hasn't got a case of dry rot," smiled Drew. "What other magic have you performed?"

"Even the cars have changed," Jean went on, encouraged. "Instead of the old, black, dirty Volkswagons, there've been shiny silver Volvos on the lot. There's so many expensive cars racing too fast in town, they have all the townspeople disgusted. The little village is spilling over with people."

"You've been doing something about that new little girl, that phenomenon from the East. I've heard something about her, though I haven't heard her yet." Drew leaned on a sawhorse left at the entrance. This was the closest talk she and Jean had exchanged since the accident. Drew was almost never without Karen.

"Yes, right. Now she's with her mother in Santa Maria. But, we're signing her up. She's going to work here. I listened to her in L.A. and heard her recently at John Hancock in Santa Maria."

"Say, soon, I'd like to hear her. Maybe I could teach a couple of lessons a week. Say, has somebody been keeping you busy of late? Up a lot of late nights. People have been telling me . . ." she looked at Jean out of the corner of her eye.

"Hey, that's nothing I want to talk about."

"Taking a lot of energy, is he? They say he's some friend of this child prodigy."

"Who's been ratting on me? If you mean David, he's been doing the publicity on this child for a year now. You mean David, he's a publicist, very different. Interested in theater. Books, too."

"I hear he's quite presentable. Everybody's met him. They say he's been climbing your stairs a lot lately." Drew had a twinkle in her eye. "You mustn't get too exhausted. I'd be forced to run the school by myself."

This was the first real conversation they had shared for weeks. Jean was more than comfortable in the quizzing. It had been a natural consequence for her to get to know David, as well as Aurora and Mrs. Jacobson, to get things settled. It had certainly brought her out of her moodiness. She sighed. This place is too packed together, no privacy.

Drew flashed her a winning smile. "Funny. No wonder nobody gets any work done here until noon."

Jean felt she had pushed at her. "Come on now, look at all we've done in three months, and without you."

"Don't be miffed. I'm just testing your feelings."

At noon, strains of music were heard over the two-acre compound. They were setting up in the practice rooms. A string quartet was performing on the 31st. Usually, things didn't get to full action until one in the afternoon. Everyone practiced in the mornings.

Every day there were 50 to 100 people involved in the compound. Twenty or so cars drove up and down the drive. Some elderly virtuosos with streaming silver hair mingled with dozens of twenty-year-old students.

On a chance meeting, the girl Aurora was brought in to have Drew listen to a brief concerto. Anjelica Jacobson was in the practice room with Jean and Drew. The notes from the expensive piano in the conservatory were mature, unexpected from a child of eleven. Already the child had a thick mane of coarse, black hair.

"Did you talk with Jean? Is it agreed that you could leave Aurora to live with us at the compound?" Drew was asking that the child become a permanent resident. They had offered her a scholarship knowing what an asset the prodigy would be to the school.

"I'd hate to leave her, but I have little choice. I have to work over in Santa Maria. There's just a studio apartment for the two of us. I could come up by bus on weekends."

The arrangement was made. Jean escorted Anjelica Jacobson back in her own car, a curious look in her eye. Could Mrs. Jacobson really bear to part with Aurora, leave her like an orphan? Still, it was in Llangolen that Aurora could receive the training she needed. The mother couldn't expect to saddle the school with two extra people to feed. Jean took the two of them to Santa Maria with the idea that the following week Mrs. Jacobson would bring her daughter to stay in one of the twin-doored cottages. The girl was to eat in the main dining hall. And her mother could visit on weekends.

By the following Monday, Aurora was established into a routine of lessons, practicing six hours a day. She fitted naturally into the compound; her personality was strong enough to survive those dominant egos.

One morning Jean grabbed a moment and sat listening to beautiful notes drifting out from the cypress trees.

"Wonder what that is...?"

"I think a Mozart, maybe. Yes, Fifth Concerto in B."

The practice rooms rang with cello and violin. At night, young women brought in electric guitars. The second Music Festival coming up in July bisected the school session which got notice from the eastern states. Every week some new woman would appear who had gone to Julliard; she wanted to look over their facilities. There was a master teacher for each instrument. Jean was forced to hire a main cook from the town, together with two kitchen helpers; still, Hans and Gretyl kept the reception and the tap room open at the entrance. A food entree was catered in from the outside, and the cook prepared the rest of the evening meal.

Aurora fitted in happily, seeing her mother each weekend. Jean had the mother over for tea. Anjelica Jacobson was attractive, though somewhat worn. She was feminine, but distress and worry for money was in her eye. Her husband had been a music conductor in the south of Denmark, but circumstances adversely forced Anjelica to provide a living for herself and her gifted daughter, so they had emigrated to the States. Aurora loved being with her mother. She enjoyed dictating her. She also loved all the attention she was getting from music people at the compound.

Jean asked Anjelica one day, "Do you mind leaving your daughter when you go back to Santa Maria?"

"No," Anjelica looked up in a serene way from a dress hem, "I know this is best. This way you can give her..."

"Her chance for fame."

"Yes, here she has a piano, excellent instruction, and most especially, she has her board and keep. I can't do it. I can barely take care of myself in one room. I barely have enough bus fare to come down here."

Jean made a note to herself sometime to drive Anjelica back in her car to save her a bus trip. It would be on Jean's way to Santa Barbara. What seemed natural was the comfortable way they all sat together in Hans' tap room. Gretyl would come sit down, and they made a foursome.

I'm comfortable, Jean thought, having talked with nothing but workmen all day.

David McClintock was away in New York. Somehow when the five of them were together, a rivalry sprang up.

"Relieved?" smirked Drew at Jean. "You looked kinda worn out, a few too many late nights. It's a big thing, having a boyfriend . . ."

"Sure is a big thing, especially with David," Jean looked embarrassed, and she looked toward the door. That was the only veiled allusion to David's physicality. Jean was glad enough that Drew was settled and stable and didn't feel she had to make prying comments.

Now at the table, Jean asked Anjelica if Aurora was ready for the first recital.

Anjelica responded, more to herself than to Drew. "She's been ready for a year. She can do this as part of her routine work. As her mother, I've kept her professionally practicing six to seven hours each day." Then Anjelica's face relaxed, as if some powerful work had been completed.

The town of Llangolen was aware of Aurora's presence on the hill. Few of the townspeople had come to the compound, but they wondered about the talented child. They heard about her and read about her. One or two locals wandered into the recital and sat there stony-faced. The day of the recital, the school received an unexpected press from L.A. David McClintock had done his work expertly, and Charles Champlin had driven up. The piece proclaimed they had a rising star on their hands. The town read the paper and stirred again about such notoriety.

Drew hadn't expected so much publicity; it took her by surprise.

The length of the article attracted attention to them as the second festival time approached. There was a hubbub in the night activity as people swelled the town. The late night summer fog had started, and a summer haze covered the normal blue of the V leading down to the sea. Mrs. Jacobson came up one foggy morning with the dress for Aurora.

"Will you see to it, Jean, that she gets transportation to L.A., either you and David, or just you?" Drew asked Mrs. Jacobson to go because there was a TV interview by Jack Scheidt for a national show. "Got to get her there early Saturday. Hard to get there because it's at ten in the morning."

"David's away. And don't you need me here since the festival's in a week?"

"Oh, come on. I'm in great shape now, and I have Karen and Gretyl to help. No, we need you to help do this. Go with Anjelica and Aurora."

"Of course, I'll take care of it." Jean was comfortable and glad to be with Anjelica. And she knew L.A.

"Better stay overnight. I don't think you can get there starting extremely early in Llangolen. It's a five-hour drive."

"Yeah, well, five hours there for the interview and the same back. I want to be here for Saturday night."

Drew pressed a question that had been bothering her. "This publicity David's been giving us will be the making of us. You'd better keep him around. He's excellent. By the way, how much has been going on between you?"

Jean blushed. They had never discussed this.

"Well, you gonna marry him?"

"He's not a permanent person. He flies off to all continents for his work. We're not exactly mated, you know."

"What's in it for you? I'm not directing..."

"You're not directing my life for me. No, the school maybe, but not me," Jean was snappish. Drew had become too personal; she wasn't letting her into her own thoughts too much. Drew had too much of a need to control. She wanted to be the one who knew what to do. It was ignominious for Jean because she was so much older.

Drew retreated to safety. "Getting back to the weekend trip, get a motel for Friday night. I'm having to answer these letters about Aurora. Julliard seems interested, but I wonder if the New York scene would be good for her."

"I thought Aurora was happy here."

"I know she is. Plenty of people to smother her, and the study conditions are far less hectic."

Drew was beginning to be possessive of their prize. Jean knew that Drew had no intention of letting her name slip away.

Jean sneaked in a sly dig. "Besides, you love her, we all love her. I think you pay more attention to her than you do to Karen," she darted it back at Drew.

"I think it's good business for us. She's worthy of direction. She's growing, and I believe she will have international scope. I'm convinced that she is a genius. Next year, I'm going to try to line up a Stanford connection. If I could work out two lessons a month with Berkwitz, her future would be assured."

"Well, I'm glad you can handle her. Sometimes she seems so conceited and self-serving. I can't stand it, especially the way she snaps and controls her mother." Jean got a burr off her chest in letting her feelings out.

Drew sighed, "Sometimes she is a pain, but I've noticed you don't find Anjelica a pain."

"Knock it off, she's someone close to my age I can talk to," she said with emphasis on the last statement.

July swept down on them. Tourists swarmed all over town, the regular summer people and, soon, the arrivals for their weekend made discussion impossible. The hard question was where to put everybody. They had to expedite housing because journalists and reporters were arriving from all over the country. Many newspapers wanted to find out what the excitement was about here. This time Jean and Drew got plenty of national coverage, but for now the question was how could they accommodate everyone? The few hotels in town quickly filled. The resort on the hill packed in people, and some others had to go to private homes.

David McClintoch came into town for the weekend with his customary sweeping energy. He managed his way into every dormitory trying to pick up facts about the performers. Rumor was that he tried to pick up a few women to go out under the pines with him.

"I love these intelligent women with long necks, long waists, long fingers," David admitted to Jean. The quantities of young women excited him. They, on the other hand, were not so stimulated. Some were a little annoyed by his advances. He was like a sparrow picking up twigs for a nest. Once in awhile he was successful, but most of the time these young musicians were resentful. He was an annoyance, taking them away from their practice time.

Jean, too, began to resist his insidious pressure to direct her own personal activities.

Sometimes he would rush up the steps, overwhelming her and forcing his way into the apartment. He didn't have many preliminaries to his love-making. He would press her to him, force her back onto her small window seat and, in about ten minutes, he'd be off and down the stairs again. Jean didn't really respond to him sexually, but she put up with it because he was so filled with information. And he could help the school.

Another thing she objected to was his lordly approach to solving all her problems. He wanted to tell her about running the school. He put a subtle negative pressure on her that was hard to put a finger on. She had to resist such control.

One day something happened that distressed her. She was surprised to find him inside Aurora's room where the eleven-year-old was looking at him in surprise.

"What are you doing here, David? Aurora never has anyone in here except her mother."

"I'm getting the information for the article. And I was just telling her what great hair she has." David stroked the glossy hair, but Aurora pulled away and retreated.

"I don't think you should come in Aurora's room. Don't do that again," remonstrated Jean. But David didn't seem to be rebuffed and went off with his usual brashness.

Aurora was being inspected from all sides. For the two days of the festival all students were released from their daily practice house, and Aurora's mother found it necessary to leave her job in Santa Maria to take closer supervision of her daughter. Many people were taking interviews as some sort of curiosity, and Aurora needed to have someone watching out for her. This jeopardized Mrs. Jacobson's job security, but for the time being, it couldn't be helped. Jean told her they would try to find her work closer into Llangolen and, for now, she would simply stay with Aurora.

Mrs. Jacobson left her few belongings, including her sewing machine in Santa Maria and came to stay with all the rest in the compound. She stayed in the same cubicle with Aurora. Anjelica, Hans, and Jean would meet in the tap room where they would gather after dinner; it was their only social time.

The festival date appeared.

The wild activity of the two days and Friday night as well, came to a climax on the Saturday and continued into Sunday. By Monday most of the groups had packed up, leaving two rock groups there to stay for Monday night.

The people of Llangolen seemed relieved to be rid of them all. Even though it was good for business, the festival people were regarded as strange intruders. The people had started to mutter to themselves about how many women there were in the enclave, so few men. And the prize pupil, why was it she was being brought up among so many women? Why didn't she go to the regular school in Llangolen? Some of the teachers in the lower school in town promoted such grumbling. The child was a celebrity by this time, but how was she learning her writing and geography? For the most part, these negative remarks were kept hidden from Drew and the others.

Meanwhile, the Monday after the Festival was over, all practice rooms gave off the strains of music from eleven in the morning until seven at night. The summer term was continuing. Beautiful weather contributed to the general comfort of studying and concentration on careers.

In the United States institutions where specialization in music training is done, it is in connection with regular college and university study, in departments. Llangolen now was beginning to get some students who were wanting to ignore general education and simply improve along their own specialization.

Drew had a hard time getting wind instrument teachers and a tuba teacher, but they had a synthesizer and several of the musicians knew electric guitar. During this time of high activity, she was able to contact new teachers. Just as regular practice days began to be the normal expectation, a gust of fresh dissension came up from the town. Now there was insinuating talk about the propriety of raising a young girl exclusively in the company of women. It took a while for Drew to get the full impact, but one of the women in town seemed to be at the root of it. Drew knew there would be trouble for the school if such talk continued.

CHAPTER FIFTEEN

A Prophesy Comes True

For a time, harmony was established in the days following the midsummer concert. But it was not lasting. The town had been pulled into a tired frazzle by extra visitors. The businessmen began to mutter to each other about having so much publicity. The locals felt that too many strange people had been asking for hard-to-get luxuries. Real resentment began to rise up against Aurora who was the target. What was so great about an eleven-year-old girl? Two of the villagers came up to the first recital. One of them, Mrs. McGrag, could not stand having someone new as the object of so much attention. She detested anything that she couldn't understand, or anyone whose thinking was unconventional.

Why was this young girl living solely in the company of women? Mrs. McGrag began some rumors. More negative talking and grumbling broke out in her small coterie. She didn't have too many friends since long days before she had many times caused trouble in the town's school.

Thirty years ago, Mary McGrag had gone to the University of California at Berkeley where she had been involved with intellectuals speaking of Communist and Socialist ideals. She had been intertwined with that group and had joined in the thinking that many of the world's ills are caused by greed of the few. Mrs. McGrag came to this community, and everywhere she looked she saw Communists. By the age of thirty, she developed a condition diagnosed as epilepsy. She had grand mal attacks. She raised a ruckus at every meeting she went to. Then she would have an attack, resulting in shocks to her brain, and as a result, ideas she had formulated in her youth became fixed and obsessive. Her face became a mask with harsh lines between her brows and on either sides of her mouth. When something that was fresh came into town, she felt obligated to get to the bottom of the new enthusiasm and root it out. Maybe she merely was jealous of the young.

When she saw that Drew was the key figure of the school, she focused all her hatred on her. Drew had changed her image because of all the visitors and their cameras that had come in July. She started to wear dresses, expensive ones, every day instead of her broad-wale corduroys. On a certain day, she would be seen in a long coatdress over slim, skintight pants, her legs encased in violet, with stiletto-heeled pumps on her feet. She looked like a model out of *West Coast Vogue.* The young schoolboy look was gone and, tall as she was, she looked like a starlet. Mrs. McGrag targeted all her morbid speculations on Drew and marshalled forces of her own friends to make Aurora an object of scandal. What was going on at this school? She raised questions around town until she got two other women in with her to demand that they all be allowed to observe the auditorium and conservatory. They wanted to attend lessons and look at housing. By September, she had permission. Before that time, she was going to walk in unannounced.

Most of the eighteen permanent residents at Llangolen noticed a change in the way they were treated in the town. The locals felt suspicious that something unholy was going on above the hill. The shop owners sullenly served baked goods and groceries. Twice the women of Llangolen were refused gas at the local station.

Finally, Drew decided she had to face the situation.

"What could be her official position?" Jean inquired of Drew.

Drew was dressed in a purple slouch vinyl jacket over a linen white shell, brown leather skirt and sleek brown hose. She draped four feet of leg over the Morris chair. Her shoulders shrugged, "Doesn't have any. I think she wants attention and can't stand all of us getting it."

Jean pursued the question. "This Mrs. McGrag, what's she got to do with music? What empowers her?"

"I'm sure she has no title. She has a few townswomen worked up, probably some lonely people with some years on them, people who need to fill up their lives." Drew wasn't fearful, but she sensed that a tedious scene might be ahead.

"Do you think she's got it in for you, Drew?"

"Someone said Mary McGrag hated single women."

"Hmmmmph! Could be it's love. Probably a suppressed dyke," snorted Jean. "Anyhow, she is coming on a visit. Tomorrow. Something about how Aurora's living."

Drew thought again, "Hey, maybe we could let Aurora's mother handle part of this. In any case, don't allow David to blow this up out of proportion in some news article."

"David! Listen, we've got trouble with David. Do you know what happened two days ago with Aurora?"

"No, I know nothing about it."

"I walked into Aurora's apartment just in time to see David in there with our young prodigy, and she said to me... 'I'm trying to get dressed. Tell him to leave because I have to go practice.' She looked down at the floor and seemed nervous. I had to walk him backwards out into the street."

"What the heck was he doing in there?" asked Drew.

"I told him he shouldn't be in Aurora's room, and he said he was merely writing a story for a release. Then I told Aurora just to see David when he was in the auditorium," Jean answered. "David's face got dark and fierce, and he disappeared. He's been rude and awful to me lately too."

Jean determined to keep constant surveillance of Aurora by the other members of the music staff.

Drew returned to the new plan. "Anyhow, as we were saying, let's let Anjelica Jacobson move in from Santa Maria, move her stuff right in there with her daughter. Take her belongings..."

"Exactly. Into that small half-apartment. It would save her money for living." Drew half slanted her eyes over at Jean. Almost too ready to agree to that, she thought, amused. How these little enthusiasms get started. David must have made her disgusted for sure.

"Anjelica would love it. She hates that secretary job anyway. We can support her since the room isn't anything for cost, and she'd be with her daughter..."

"Yes, and you..."

"Yes, and Hans...and..."

"It would block Mrs. McGrag."

"And please, you, Jean," Drew said slyly. "Do you think you could call her up?"

"Sure. I know her better than anyone else, unless maybe Gretyl could. Anjelica would be the best one to repudiate changes that there was anything improper here at the school."

Drew smiled at her broadly. "Let's work it that way."

In the meantime, Mrs. McGrag had already opened charges against the women's group on the hill. She had gone to the chief of police and to some of the child care groups about town. They were all organized to make a visitation of the conservatory. Drew made a condition in response to this call, that since the school had to maintain a schedule, no more than three visitors would be allowed into recital hall or concert room.

Mrs. McGrag appeared the next day at one o'clock, unsmiling and hostile.

Drew was there to meet her. The woman's face was set, unvarying, condemning. "We have come to see what is going on. We have heard things are irregular. Is it true that there are no prayers or services at this school?"

The rigid lines of her face and unexpressive eyes made Drew wonder whether she would hear anything said to her. The woman's thought patterns had become fixed because of damage to the brain which could not be recovered by the doctors. Additionally, she had to take a medication to prevent further attacks.

Nevertheless, her appearance was formidable and seemed to have an authoritative stamp. This had to be dealt with.

So Drew allowed her and her two women companions to go around the grounds and recital hall. They also looked in at Aurora practicing her usual Chopin in one of the side rooms. The women's faces looked red and indignant.

To Jean, who was more easily intimidated than Drew, the woman appeared to be dragon-like indeed. She carried a sizable portable tape recorder around with her that must have tested her strength. She wanted to pick up all conversations. She put the machine down, stooping to adjust her thick and dowdy nylons looped around trunk-like legs. Her eyes were fixed and black. She really did look like a monster, Jean decided. The tense feeling did not subside; these people were clearly against them. Drew explained some things, but she was not subservient to the women. Finally, the women left, with Mrs. McGrag saying, "We are coming back, and we are bringing the chief of police with us."

Seeking a relief, Jean, Drew, Karen, and Gretyl went down the cliff steps leading to the Dutch Tea Room and Bakery.

They ordered a large pot of English tea for four. Each one was given an individual clay teapot, covered in violets or cornflowers. They sat at an ice cream table in the corner while two parties of local merchants eyed them curiously. A banker and the lady who sold baskets at a filling station gave them a particularly cold, hard stare.

Drew rose to go to the counter, picked out an orange iced roll, two croissants, and a hot cross bun. Open-faced sandwiches and eclairs rested on the refrigerated turn-table glass case.

The audience also consisted of an ancient lady who had worked for Walt Disney Productions, besides the sullen others. The atmosphere was unfriendly. Drew had no intention of satisfying the morbid curiosity of these conservatives. She would prefer to be scandalous, and if she appeared immoral, the happier she would be.

She made her back slouchy and insolent as she regained the table, conscious that every eye had been on her. "Who are these horrible people bothering us?"

"They say they want to put us on a radio station to gain exposure of Llangolen Music School," Gretyl answered.

"Let them, hang it. It will give us more publicity. Be good for our side," Drew said this into the scowly cheeks of the banker. He let his fierce eyebrows come back to their normal level.

"By *them,* you mean that gargoyle of a woman? With the two friends she's got?" Karen backed her up.

Drew could tell they were picking up on their conversation. The place was too small not to overhear. Finally, the banker gave a scrape to his chair and got up in disgust.

"What in heaven's name do they think we're doing to Aurora?"

The accusations had seemed so amorphous that the people on the hill couldn't put a finger on it. But Drew knew they meant something sinister and unnatural. All the child development people thought it wrong to bring up a child without a father somewhere around. Besides, their whole household was an enclave of women.

The next evening the weather turned dark and stormy with slanting rain coming in the French doors and windows. A telephone call came through reception, the only interruption from the sound of the rain.

"They say they are sending a TV photographer from Santa Maria. They want to take pictures of Aurora," Gretyl reported, while sharp crackles came down the wire from the east end of town. The voice, which was sympathetic, belonged to a man who knew both sides of the controversy as well as the history of Mrs. McGrag.

"They think we are here to scandalize the innocents," Drew was excited. She called back, "Let them come. It isn't the right publicity, but it will draw public attention." Nobody seemed to fear the intrusion; in fact, they welcomed it.

By the next week, the counterforces had gathered enough strength to get some TV coverage. The newsmen entered just as the first fall concert was beginning, and the excitement mounted, drawing dozens of curiosity seekers who might not have attended. David added to the confusion, seeming to enjoy elaborating on the reports and feeding them strange information. Jean found herself more annoyed than comforted by his presence. He was insolent to her. He ignored everything she said.

"David, you don't have to criticize what I am wearing," Jean told him. But David continued to be somewhat hateful to her and, after awhile, she began to think he was working at counterpurposes to the school.

The program went off quite well, though a few hecklers remained at the gate. The next morning when Mrs. McGrag reappeared, this time with an immense tape recorder clutched in both arms, Drew decided to shut down their efforts to discredit the school.

"You simply cannot enter," Drew declared as she faced a staring set of black eyes. "If you're not enrolled in one of our courses, you can't come in here," and she closed the concert hall door an inch from Mary McGrag's face.

The horrible face made no movement. She studied Drew impassively. Then Mrs. McGrag's foot shoved forward, encountering Drew's knee.

"No, I mean it. Get out."

"But I've never been pushed out of any public building before." Mrs. McGrag still sounded official, but Drew knew that others had ousted her before.

"That's just what you say. Now get out!"

"I'm getting on the radio and letting everyone know what is really going on here. Schools shouldn't be run by women." The women didn't give up easily.

"I'll bet you can't get five people to listen to you," closed off Drew, and the woman was forced to go. Drew had stood firm and hadn't let the enemy in.

The combination of the hateful confrontations and the subsequent handling of the crisis by Drew and David's defection placed Jean more into isolation. She had a deep sense of aloneness. She had felt this way for three years, ever since that earlier disappointment. David had served to alleviate that for a time because of his dynamic contact with the outer world, but that was over. When she finally was alone for three days, she had to escape down to Hans in the tap room. Usually Aurora was practicing at night, so sometimes Mrs. Jacobson would come in to sit an hour at one of the tables.

David was still around, but Jean was annoyed with him. He would chase her up to her apartment. He seemed to be one of those men who always had something in his pocket. Poor David. He was convinced that he was invincible with women, but Jean thought that he simply wasn't sexually attractive. Women didn't find him appealing.

One afternoon she was idly leaning against her sun porch windows going through papers. Her eye caught at a level which led right across into Drew's and Karen's upstairs living room. A corner view led directly into the sectional couch. Jean caught sight of what could have been David, standing upright. What was he doing in there? Then she caught a glimpse of hair, must have been Karen's hair. She realized with a shock that he was forcing Karen to have sex with him. A struggle was going on. Karen had never shown interest in David.

She saw that David had his knees pressed down on something. It must have been Karen's stomach, and her skirt was pulled up to her waist. Jean could see her bare legs twisted to the left. They both disappeared for an instant, and then Karen lunged across the room, but came back up then against the closed windows.

Jean thought she ought to get help at the Bearcat Bookstore, but what if Karen had asked him up there?

At this point, she had a flash of hatred for David. She realized that during the past weeks, he had forced her more than once. He had an antagonistic cold manner, disdainful. Jean felt disregarded, taken for granted. She had tried to be herself, discussing the publicity and news of the school, but she realized now that he didn't have any interest in her conversation.

Suddenly, the front door of Drew's apartment burst open. David broke the handle of the screen door, jumped down the flight of stairs, two at a time, and disappeared around the corner into his car. Jean waited a moment, then she went to see what had happened to Karen who was crying bitterly. Her skirt was unbuttoned and turned backwards. She looked at Jean, swearing, "He came in on me suddenly, telling me he just had to talk to me, that he'd heard about a permanent job for me so I could stay in town longer. I believed him. Then he said, 'Let's try it like this,' and he folded my arms behind my back and pressed himself down on top of me. My God, that thing must be fourteen inches! He grabbed my skirt up before I knew what he was after. Wait'l . . ."

"Drew hears about this?" supplied Jean. She knew Karen was ashamed. And she, herself, had been too surprised to do anything. She couldn't very well say things out because it would discredit her and David's relationship, but Jean thought, how do I explain that I was a voyeur or something? By the time I started to do anything, there was David stomping down the stairs. What was I supposed to say? "I'm here behind my bamboo curtain?"

Jean felt inadequate, more separate than ever. She guessed she'd let Karen handle it with Drew. This was up to her. And she, Jean, was mad at David.

I really must do something about David, she thought.

Enraged. Drew was furious when she heard about the attack on Karen. After so much had been happening, all she wanted to do was giggle and finally enjoy life. It had been a struggle to get the new school going; then the accident had happened; it seemed that someone was always twisting their mooring lines. Now this onslaught against her friend. Everything was so ambiguous. Why had

Karen asked David in to their apartment? Her motivation was suspicious, and now there was some strained feeling between them. A sort of paranoia had set in, just a misunderstanding, everything askew.

"Why wasn't I invited to that meeting about the next interview of Aurora two nights ago?" Karen demanded.

Drew replied, "You weren't really involved, and I didn't bother to say anything to you. It was about news reporters. Also, you were down in the Bearcat with some other announcement."

"I'm just on the sidelines. Besides, you're spending too much time with that little girl. You're sort of enthralled. She's running the whole show. She's acting like the boss, instead of some child."

"Well, I think Aurora's being a part of Llangolen will put this place on the map."

"I think you're putting her in first place in everything," and Karen stamped out.

Drew continued to develop publicity about Aurora's genius, traveling to L.A. to arrange the next public exposure of Aurora. Karen could complain, Drew thought, but Drew was in control of her own plan of action.

As the days passed, Karen began to speak of returning to her native Toronto.

"What for? It's too cold up there."

"Yes, but I can continue my education. I want to do something for *me*. I think I have more of a future there than around Llangolen. Besides, they're telling me my replacement semester is at an end; the professor is coming back in January. I'm just thinking about it, that's all."

In the interim, David had finished himself at Llangolen. He was becoming unwelcome. The last two news releases had been sarcastic and slighting, almost denigrating to the school. It wasn't even subtle. David continued to mention Aurora in the releases, but when he was present, the women watched him very closely. He was never given a chance to be with Aurora alone, and Karen he avoided.

Jean was embarrassed by the assault against Karen. She felt more alone than ever. Three years had elapsed since she had felt emotion for anyone. She had felt so betrayed. Now she realized that she had lost a trusted friend. David was taking her for granted, that was it. When he came around the compound now to write up his stories, he went right to the tap room, had a few beers and talked over the incident. They would cast sly glances at David, joking about the anatomy below the waist. Discussing his biological endowment, they would make references to fourteen, David's proud number.

"Isn't Aurora getting close to fourteen now?" one would say.

"No, still twelve," and giggle as they looked in David's direction.

"What is that dress size, fourteen?" . . . and . . . "Fourteen days till Christmas." And David felt the derision slanted toward him. Finally Christmas approached, and by that time, Drew had made a major breakthrough for the young prodigy. The other women had gotten together in their rage against David. At last, one of them got indignant and ran him off the school limits.

CHAPTER SIXTEEN

The Center Unfolds

Jean continued to be of the party, but she didn't really feel close to anyone there. When the biggest bunch of them got really drunk, she slipped out down the kitchen steps and climbed up to her own apartment.

One of the elements of the friendship was that Drew never considered Jean as worthy of having a boy friend (or girl friend). Anybody wanting her that way, or the idea of "dating" never occurred to her about Jean. David had been around. Well, what did that mean? All she knew from the past was that Jean had had a disappointment around three years before showing up in their new location. Immersed in her own lover, the thought that Jean might be lonesome never entered her mind. She didn't want to think of her that way, anyway. Maybe down underneath, she wanted Jean to be solitary and always there for her.

Throughout the fall, new people came to the conservatory to listen or perform. As this fall season changed, so did the clientele. Llangolen became the rage of the coast, and they were "discovered" by Santa Barbara musicians and teachers from Stanford. Aurora also took on a charisma of her own.

The physical facility increased in sophistication because of the influx. Gretyl and innkeeper Hans were obliged to put in extra food in the tap room, tasty pizza surprises covered with perfectly ripe tomato slices covered with basil, chunky slices of mozzarella and a drizzle of oil. They had to supply New York crust. "Ya wanna some anchovies this time?" And Gretyl created a spinach pie that could be sold in slices.

As a result of the increased traffic of ambitious, bright people, Drew changed her apartment, painted her staircase a marble green with rich runners of brown carpet. She had an artist paint her window shades. The compound itself became more worldly and suitable to the New York or San Francisco people.

Drew was now fully recovered from her accident. She was able to don jodhpurs to go horseback riding up Park Hill with Aurora or one of the Santa Barbara theater people. She was in total control of her health, and every day she would bicycle with one or two others. She bought tight black cycling pants and went out three or four times a week. She had so much in her life that even Karen was being neglected.

"Where are you going today? I thought we were going to eat seafood." But Drew was putting together a wicker hamper full of French bread sandwiches loaded with celery hearts, pitted black olives and tuna salad. She added a thermos of hot water to make her coffee at the picnic spot. She then loaded half of a dark chocolate cake.

"I have to go with this music critic. From Chicago. I just have to get this article done with her, and I thought I'd show her Sebastian and probably one tier of Hearst."

"But what about me? I'd sorta . . . I never see you . . ."

"Got to do this. It's business. Put us on the map with the Midwest connection."

"I thought we'd go down to the pier."

"Ah, hah! Suppose so, dinner there, after I get done with this."

She swung her shoulder-length blonde pageboy past Karen's face. Karen caught a breath of a new subtle perfume, and her blouse over some stone-washed jeans was slightly revealing.

Drew's inward thoughts showed her confusion and ambiguous feelings toward Karen and the new changes in her life. Muttering half under her breath, she came out with, "I'd rather dress down in old clothes and go to the wharf for some lobster thermador at the Galley. Actually, to be truthful, I want to take Aurora along with this interview person up to the northern coast, but Aurora is practicing. I need to get a line on a notable engagement, either Midwest or on the Southern Coast. Heck!" She yelled out loud, so that Karen could hear. "I feel horribly pulled, do you see?"

"Don't forget to fill me in between the rest of your people," her insidious dig at Drew was noticed. "Three-thirty or four, okay?"

Then Drew set her thought deliberately toward delivering the goods of a full-length article to appear in the Chicago Music Section pages. She felt capable. She knew she was getting better at arranging the publicity since David's defection. She didn't write it; Jean wrote it. The school now was at high tempo. She was having exciting days, and her face showed it. She glowed with health. But she wished Karen could program her own life so that she wouldn't have to feel guilty. What was Jean doing, too, she wondered. But soon, under the pressure of the time deadline, she swung the hamper into the van and forgot about Karen.

The next major happening was that *Vanity Fair* reporters, two of them, came out for a week to do a full article on them.

I'm so delighted, Jean thought, that I'm not spending a life like my parents, or most midwesterners whose quality of life depends mostly on the state of the weather and the mundane details of what was going to be for lunch or dinner. I would die of intellectual starvation, she thought. She had heard them, people of her own kind, go on for hours... "Well, did they get a gully washer down at Perham?"

"Sure did, nothing over here at Frazee, barely a sprinkle. Need it. The gardens are dry. Yep, we got about four inches in an hour, I heard. Real downpour."

"Yes, well, how was it when you drove your truck over to Buck's Mills?"

"Hardly a drop. Just went in the beer joint and had me one beer. Not a drop of rain. Yessir. They sure do need it."

This line of talk could take up about ten to fifteen minutes without going under the surface of their brains. There was no depth to their thinking. If they did suffer emotionally, nobody talked out loud about it. Drew reflected on the mediocrity of their lives, the absence of anything artistic or lasting. It was all about...the family, too, she added. Everything revolved around the immediate family. My family, I love them...but...look at the fullness of my life here, the fascinating quality of life that I'm getting here in this quaint village. I would have died of emotional and mental starvation.

"What now?" groaned Drew in despair. Some things at Llangolen were not all roses and geraniums. "This again?"

For ten days now they had been struggling with plumbing and drain problems. One of the joys of an old set of buildings was refurbishing pipes and pumps dating back to the early fifties.

"You'll have to get the well man again."

"What? He's been here three times."

"I think he's in love with you and looking for an excuse to come back."

"I think he's in love with our money."

The same day the toilets refused to flush in the long shed dormitories. Jean was rung in on the fixit department.

"I know, I know. That pump has been running on and off all night. Drives me crazy. I haven't been able to sleep over here. I can hear it from here."

"How come you're up at night? You never come over for a drink."

"I know, but I want to get some writing done, and you're always talking about music or biking." Jean let her have it just where it was.

"Why don't you get some writing types over here? I understand writers have been known to drink a bit."

"You might have an idea there. Getting kinda short of communication with someone who talks my language." But Jean was doubtful of Drew's pretense to help her.

She got the pump fixed so that it wouldn't labor so hard at night, but when that was fixed, all the toilets in the longshed dormitory, plus the Bearcat Bookstore, got stuffed up. When the plumber unearthed a toothbrush out of it, that helped the situation, but they weren't out of trouble by a long way.

"Guess what now, Drew?"

"I'm about filled to the top on this sanitation business. I want to spend money on French horns."

"Better spend it on French hip baths instead. Look now, we have to tie in with the town's sewer system, and an entire new set of tanks and pipes dug on the edge of the hillside and toed in with the main pipe," Jean let her have the whole bad news.

"And you know those beds up there? The previous types must have weighed 300 pounds. There's a hole in each 'Will not Sag' springs that you lose your whole body in."

"What'll we do about that?" Drew looked beseechingly at Jean. "Just hire fat mamas around here?"

"We have to get box springs and mattresses," she grinned. "And

I'd advise enrolling only girls with toothpick figures from now on. More of your visiting Easterners ought to be svelt. Those people think 'roughing it' is out West in some Holidrome where the room is glassed over with the swimming pool and a place where you order your prime rib served at poolside."

"They'll have to put up with what we have here." Drew had her hands full trying to entertain the demanding visitors from Manhattan. They wore sophisticated clothes, black velvet narrow pants with slightly belled legs on top of black patent leather heels, black shell tops, really elegant clothes compared to Western wear. Their taste in food was also demanding. One of the women bought an expresso coffee pot in the University Coffee Expresso Cafe because she was used to having steamed coffee in the morning. She had just completed brewing a pot in the conservatory receiving hall when Aurora came prancing in for her early morning practice. "Want some?" asked the thirty-three-old woman named Francesca.

"Sure," answered Aurora and went bounding backstage to get a round bowl to drink it in. She poured out *all* the coffee into her bowl and sat there drinking it. When Francesca came back into the room she asked...

"Where's my cup?"

"Well, I drank it." Aurora looked down at the remainder in her large bowl, a little line of brown around her mouth. "Here, you can have the rest."

"No thanks," returned Francesca who turned on her heel and flounced out. Incidents like this gave Aurora the reputation of an enfant terrible. Also, the lack of facilities made Llangolen seem barbarian. The people would simply have to adjust to the ways of the West thought Drew, and she shrugged it off, plumbing and all.

Still, Drew thought, she was having an excitingly-lived time. And in a way, she resented being so constricted by Karen, who was depressed. "Why should I be dragged down because she is on a bummer time of her life? This is peak for me, unless there's more to come. I want to holler and sing. Above all, I want to laugh, yes, and have drinks with my friends. But Karen wants me to spend all my time with her, and she's short of money just having this part-time post. She isn't sure where the next job will come. Heck, I'm not going to be dragged down by it. I'm going to swing a bit, not going to get my spirits down. I've come through all that worried time."

After voicing some of this aloud to her friends, Drew would hold a dinner party in her own dining room. She would put on Wagner at the highest volume on the stereo. One night she did a mock conductor's scene from "The Flight of the Valkeries" with a stolen chopstick she had taken from a restaurant down south, Wolfgang Puck's in Santa Monica. Her elegant friends, sophisticatedly dressed, seemed a little confused, but kept pace with the music, but Karen, sitting back quietly, seemed out of her element, backward with the conversation, as though she had grown up sheltered, rural, which she had in Canada. As the drinks before dinner and the wine flowed, Karen watched, bewildered, uneasy in the company. She stared, mute, as her friend, clad in white jodhpurs, dropped her shirt as she continued to conduct the orchestra. Karen was shocked. A one-shouldered blouse would have been daring enough, but she felt a betrayal of intimacy.

Drew...well, it wasn't really Drew's fault, thought Karen. When she thought out her personality, she always had to feel she knew what was in, the best people, that there was someone to dominate. A strong person was needed as a foil for such a strong ego, and Karen didn't feel that strong. She felt dowdy and unappreciated. Unloved. There, it was out in the open. She felt overridden and, therefore, was on her way out.

Karen picked up her drink and left the dining room to sit on the back sunporch. So why cry about it? Here was Drew, very successful. Both women were talented. Drew was simply outgrowing her at this point. This must happen to many professionals she reflected. Karen was glad she wasn't emotionally overwhelmed so that she couldn't see through that. But the idea of being second to these new friends had taken seed to her mind. All that was left was for a small incident to trigger a confrontation. So when the drinks and the party music ended that night, she said nothing, but withdrew into herself to reason what she should do. Their time of being together had come to an end. Christmas was approaching, a difficult time at best to reason how people felt about each other. In January, she would have to be in a different place, pursuing her own destiny. The place obviously was Toronto because she had nowhere else to go.

Drew never considered that Jean might possibly need a partner. In fact, she never thought of it at all. She was surprised when she found out the time with David had been a sexual relationship. Some of Jean's other liaisons she knew about, but that had been so far in the past that she viewed Jean as beyond it all. The fact that people would sometimes be present in Jean's apartment didn't mean anything more than casual companionship. Some people who were Jean's friends, she dismissed as "inappropriate." She thought of them as rivals for her, Drew's demands of friendship. Mostly theirs was a business attachment of long standing. There was a rift between them, she figured. But I have new friends and I'm moving on, she concluded. I have these Santa Barbara and bigger music people. Maybe I no longer need to have her listen to me while I try to puzzle things out. Gosh darn it, why does she have to be so literary and reclusive? Beside the sequinned blouse of an elegant friend from out of town, Jean did look dowdy. She looked tomboyish as she sat with her jeans legs crossed. Anjelica was sitting in the basket chair, sewing.

Drew spoke pointedly, "Clothes really do make the man, you know. They are important," she announced to Jean, primarily. "Don't you agree, Anjelica?"

Jean was embarrassed to be so criticized in front of someone she liked.

"What's wrong with what I have on?"

"Really, dolly, it hasn't style. You haven't done your fingernails, your face should have blusher on, mascara, shine your teeth. . . ."

"Gosh, isn't anything right?"

"Nobody's going to notice you unless you get a little flashy, have Curt do your hair. That super beveled cut you have could grow out and he would handle that awkward stage."

Drew really did like her friend and wanted to think she was helping her, but underneath the unwanted suggestions was a deep need to dominate. Secretly, she was a little in awe of her friend. Basically, everyone wants to come out looking good, so she lorded it over her friend.

The year ended on this impending split between the friends.

Drew spent more time with Aurora. Karen and Jean were feeling unwanted by Drew and the new circle of friends.

CHAPTER SEVENTEEN

The Monster Is Gone

The other change in atmosphere was in the town itself. It lightened up so far as the repressive Mrs. McGrag was concerned. The people who were working in businesses started to smile at Drew, and she even found herself being the object of congratulatory remarks. They were glad that she had been strong with Mrs. McGrag and had fended her off. She had been a scourge to the area for more than ten years, it came out. She was a dragon lady, indeed. They no longer felt her heat; in fact, she seemed to disappear for months to her house. Nobody saw her in town until far in the next spring, perhaps April. When they did see her, she had put on sixty pounds and had broken her leg. She was getting around with the aid of crutches. Her mighty array of friends had retreated as well. Drew thought, maybe the tale of squelching a monster had come true. At any rate, the monster and dark cloud of public opinion had dissipated into the murky depths of the Llangolen forest.

About this time, the thirteen or fourteen owners of Llangolen Music School held a big party in Drew's honor. She was having her last birthday; in fact, it was her fortieth. They got hold of helium balloons, having a party in the gardens behind the Bearcat Bookstore. Jean and Michele and Karen invited friends from Drew's previous town where she had worked, as well as most of the people involved in the whole school. Before the party began, they all to a woman took their shirts off in the garden, creating ribald slogans to include inside the balloons. Also, they put in certificates for $100 scholarships for people to trade in. They reveled there for the earlier part of the day, until the party was slated to begin and Drew's father and mother to arrive from the desert.

Drew's father did not mind anything his daughter did, and he never gave advice. Anything Drew planned was fine with him. Her father was built on the large size, over six feet, had a bluff, red face and was totally at ease with people. He was the owner of a small manufacturing company to the east of Llangolen. He was the perfect host; he would have made an innkeeper in Chaucer. Many of Drew's characteristics could be traced to him. People were comfortable with the Carl Whites.

So when Mr. White settled his big frame into the armchair in Drew's living room, he wanted to hear what all the fuss had been which had attracted the news media and been given publicity around the state.

Everyone gleefully related the attack of the dragon. Drew's mother rested on the arm of the chair, wide-eyed, smiling, housewifely. She gave a non-judgmental smile at her daughter. She never bothered about Drew's friends, but sometimes she had an unnerving habit of calling Drew up at seven in the morning just to see who would answer the phone. Usually there was some new voice.

"That's all right then . . ." Mr. White remarked after Drew had finished. "Guess you handled it by pushing back at her. That woman didn't have the numbers to support her accusations, and she just wanted people to give attention to how important she was. Good thing you have the stress off you. She didn't really sting you bad." He then made a joke about fire-breathing dragons, and Drew grinned. "Yeah, you should have smelled her breath that last day—that last time when I kicked her out of the conservatory."

Then Drew's father went on about some old World War II story about a terrible captain he had above him while learning how to fly. Mr. White still kept the old uniform—the flight jacket and the helmet with the goggles—in his closet from that time. He had trained at a small airfield close to his hometown. These articles still fitted him. Drew would have loved to keep them as vintage items, wear them to costume parties, but he was proud of them and wouldn't part with his past.

Finally, after some two and a half hours, Mr. White got up in his hearty way to say goodbye. Still vital, in his early sixties, he gave off the air of complete approval, never wanting to limit his kids and keep them from whatever they wanted to do. They went smiling down the drive, got into their large Cadillac and drove home.

Drew had been glad to see them, but now they were gone, the real party would begin, and they could be themselves. They opened the champagne, and some of the couples danced, somebody smoked a little dope.

After about two hours of that Jean sneaked down the stairs back to her own apartment, her mood falling into a depression.

CHAPTER EIGHTEEN

Jean in Limbo

A low, black mood assailed Jean. What was wrong with her? The problem, once she voiced it to herself one night, was in finding someone to talk to. She didn't have to know people with prodigious talent. To be able to absorb ideas of a person of depth like that, she would have to go on reading novels. In books, she could find the challenge she sought, but hardly ever would she be thrown into contact with a mind in full bloom. And she didn't need any more put-downs, such as Drew's. She knew that she needed someone with whom she could discuss the meaning of life, someone who could talk about literature, not literary criticism exactly, either. Come to think of it, who at the compound could discuss poetry, dissect a few lines of a really good poem? Or for that matter, have a few words of conversation following a movie? Who was there? Certainly not Hans, not David. David was far too impatient.

Then she pressed the thought further. Could any person she knew for a hundred miles around take apart a Paul Valerie poem, for instance, just picking a poet at random. Maybe I should come into contact with some people at the university, go to some poetry reading. Here I am, lost in a cacaphony of crazy musicians blowing horns—theirs. Maybe I don't need to help this outfit so much any more. Maybe I need to help myself. Well, what about Drew, her long-time buddy? She's more rational now than that time she was on drugs. That was horrible. And then she was absent in the hospital for five months. But maybe we are growing apart now; maybe she doesn't need my help quite as much.

Jean slipped into a fantasy. I need somebody to sit down with on a porch, yes, even one of those old-fashioned long verandas you read about, such as in Africa as described by Doris Lessing. I've read something like that in the readings about the Cape of Olive Shreiner.

Maybe I need to talk to a visiting author, even a resident author trying to create, even a voracious reader. So far, for two years, I have encountered none of these. Now, maybe, Jean pondered, she should make up her own world with what she wanted, stop taking orders from Drew. Something clicked in her mind. She should decide what it was she wanted, make up her own household and not be a jack-up support to someone else's dream.

In the meantime, she stayed separate, knowing she was truly alone.

The next night she again lay awake, counting the reasons for her dissatisfaction. Here I have been doing all the journalism for Aurora, writing reviews and getting them printed, yet none of the owners here care about words. No wonder there's a lack of communication with them—they care only for their music. Now I see that it is a true conflict of interest. What if my own business here is coming to an end and I am to take up my own line of work? Let's see, what was that old aphorism? "Change your attitude toward yourself and the circumstances toward you change."

I think I've done a pretty good job here. I've held the place together during these two serious illnesses, and I've helped to meld together the disparate elements of the Bearcat and the musicians. I helped do away with that monster McGrag. And for myself, I have supported my apartment here by the sea. But I still have a yearning for a real companion to talk to. I feel starved. Maybe, too, it is foolish to expect all kinds of love and good conversation from the same individual.

Well, I'm coming along, aren't I? I'm to the point of saying, "What do I want?" I think I'll try to answer that question. What about getting a real house on my own? I'd want one still in this town, but a little further apart from the other strong personalities. If I could live with someone compatible, I could have various visitors for stimulation. Then I could go on with my personal writing in addition to the same job I'm doing. All this would bring me more into contact with people who read books. That's the chief problem. Drew makes me feel diminished by her starlet appearance. I've got to improve how I look a bit, how I dress, as well as decide what simple things will make me happy.

In order, that would be: a house, here in Llangolen, with a porch, some kind of animal about, and a companion sitting somewhere in the back of the house. Now, is that so hard? That would make me happy, that would make me smile, and then I would find some true friends to talk with.

Four days later, Jean and Mrs. Jacobson found themselves devouring a chicken cooked in wine back in Jean's small sun room.

"Do you like it here, living in Llangolen, Jean?"

"I'm sort of belonging, but yet apart, if you notice how many people belong to other people."

"Judging on the basis of how I've observed you over the past months, you aren't really close to anyone. You are close to Drew and yet not. Maybe you need to know about writers."

"I hear there are some poets in town. I haven't met all of them. Gradually I'm beginning to feel cramped in this place, all shut in and subject to the organizational hoopla, but yet left out. Except for Drew."

"Drew, yes, but she has to be the outstanding one, the one everyone notices," Anjelica drew her out.

"True enough... We've been friends for seven or eight years now, but she has the main attention in this dream world that we've built."

"You mean, you were friends even when you were in that other town?" pressed Anjelica. She had an interested gleam in her eye that Jean couldn't interpret. "How'd you come to be friends?"

"Through one of those talk-out groups." Jean wondered if she might be jealous, though there was no cause. Then she decided to share her feelings of wanting something better. She embarked on the fantasy she had been creating these past few nights. "If I could get a bigger place, down the road in the eastern part of this town where there is more sunshine, maybe I would be happier. It's a little dank in this canyon, especially close to the sea."

"Want me to help you look for a place?" Anjelica fell in with her thought. "I love to look for houses. You mean you want a bigger place than this apartment?"

"Please, come along with me. Tomorrow's good. We could drive down to the end of town. I want a place where I can write. Doesn't mean it has to be bigger. Or newer. Could you go right after coffee in the morning?"

Anjelica fell in with her plan of changing residences. They didn't have an attachment other than the music school, but they shared the dissatisfactions of handling all the details.

"I don't mind most of the time, but the big heads of those egomaniacs get to be a pain," a mild complaint from Jean as they started out the next morning.

A chain of quaint shops, English or Welsh, straggled down the long arroyo of Llangolen. Tea rooms, one toy soldier shop, real estate offices and antique stores clustered in the east area where the road headed toward the highway. A few older homes sloped on the edges of hillsides, and some faced the main road. On the northside, opposite a real estate office, they spotted a yellow frame house with a complete front porch or veranda around the front and side. There, nailed to the porch, a small "For Sale" sign advertised a private phone number.

"Let's call it up, just have a brief look."

Two ancient natives of the town rolled up in a vintage Cadillac. They handed over the key. Jean and Anjelica together strolled through a house that had a charm of beveled glass and that eastern aspect of sun that Jean preferred for writing. Two bedrooms to the back completed the inside, while a low garden area ended abruptly before the hillside. The lot was small, practically no landscaping but the purple ice plant indigenous to the area, and a riot of red geraniums tumbled below the broad veranda.

"*You* could stay here and have Aurora with you," Jean broached a new area. "Perhaps she would be better away from the confusion."

"That might solve our problem with the townspeople," Anjelica looked at her rather wistfully. "Even though things were settled when Drew threw Mrs. McGrag out."

Jean wondered about Anjelica. Could that possibly be a happy look in her eye?

"Is there anything written that says you have to continue as a resident in #2 Seacroft of the Llangolen compound?" Anjelica pursued the idea a step further.

"I don't think so. It's entered into the by-laws that we can sell or trade like any other property." Jean was sure someone else could absorb her place.

"Why don't you quietly approach Drew. Then you could buy this. I could help out with your expense by paying rent money."

Jean knew that Anjelica didn't have much cash.

CHAPTER NINETEEN

A Change of Keys

She pondered over the idea for two days, then she approached Drew. Conversation about the house change had taken place between herself and Anjelica from the duplex below. This had given her a fillip, a feeling of an ally in making a change of keys. The calls were more intimate, rather conspiratory against Drew, so far as Drew's knowledge of what they were discussing.

Finally, Jean found Drew outside the compound and brought it up.

"What's the matter? You've been two days away from your house," Drew spurted out aggressively.

Jean suspected that Drew might be aware of some minor rebellion in her, some independence. No matter that Drew always wanted to shut her off. She always liked to feel that Jean was upstairs in her apartment where she could find her. Jean was behaving strangely in Drew's view, and she wasn't sure she liked it.

"Nothing is wrong, but I've got an idea I'd like to explore. I've been working on something."

"Well, I want to hear," said Drew curiously, "but I was supposed to sign papers for a new contract. I really can't talk much till tomorrow."

"No, listen to me, I want to try you out now."

"Hurry it up, then. It isn't anything about Aurora, is it? I've been working on a large contract for her. I don't want you taking her anywhere, or getting her upset."

Jean felt secure that Drew wouldn't be able to shake her confidence on this one. Out in the drive, a first winter wind started to chill their arms and to rustle the jacaranda around her door. Drew would have to face up to her new plan sometime.

"No, not taking her away, not that, you'd not be concerned that way, but..." Jean broke off, four imaginative scenes flickering in her brain, unrehearsed, but the lines set in her plan, she unfolded it into the mounting scowl on Drew's face. Drew's eyes were blue spots drilling into her own.

"Well, that wouldn't work. Aurora needs to be here to practice, just to be around us all. You can't take her off with you, nor her mother."

By now the wind was steadier and their arms were covered with goose bumps as they stood outside Jean's stairwell. They climbed up inside and sat cross-legged in the window nook. Jean renewed her cause.

"Look, Drew, I feel all cooped up here; it's so small and I can't write where there's so much happening. I need more room." Jean made her argument for independent quarters.

"What's that got to do with Aurora?"

"Anjelica Jacobson said she'd like to move in with me."

"Really!" Drew looked at her with more interest. "What's involved?"

"Nothing, only, you seem to feel you have some right. . ." Jean began.

"Not exactly, but if it affects the music school, I have a right," resistance was rigid on Drew's eyebrows and mouth.

"Won't. Just won't. It's simply an expansion, to fit my needs more," Jean's expression was dogged, her face was down.

Drew was clearly angry now and Jean would normally back down in the face of argument, but now she raised her chin.

"I just need more space to write and think. I'm thinking of getting the little yellow house at the end of Llangolen."

"I don't know where that is," Drew fumed and Jean could see two deep indentations forming between her brows.

"I know we've all been settled in the apartment cottages, but that doesn't mean we might not ever need to change," Jean's reply was doughty.

"You mean you won't stay around with us?"

"No, I don't mean that. I mean we'll be housed in the other part of town and be here during the day. We might be able to have a more normal home for Aurora."

"Do you mean that you actually plan to share this house with Aurora and Anjelica?"

"Yes, I, we do."

Drew stamped out of the apartment.

What was it between Drew and Aurora, Jean thought?

During the next month, Jean made a down payment on the yellow house. They couldn't move in until Christmas when escrow would close, but meanwhile, there was much to be done. They had to make an exit out of the compound. Karen offered to buy Jean's apartment which was located next to Drew's. That was handy as Drew's place was filled with a welter of TV interviews and music plans.

CHAPTER TWENTY

Domestic Confusion

Jean went up to Karen the next week, stuck her chin out and told her, "I'm glad you're taking my apartment in the complex."

Karen smiled gratefully. "I'd like to be closer to Drew and the others, so it's good for me, too."

"If you hadn't given me the down payment, I wouldn't have been able to buy the yellow house as soon as I have."

"You know Drew isn't happy with this new arrangement," Karen began anxiously. "She's become so close to the child."

"She wants Aurora . . ."

"To be closer in the conservatory."

"Yes," returned Jean. "But Aurora will be here practicing all day from nine until four. Anjelica Jacobson will drive her up in the mornings and stay in the half-house."

"For some reason . . ." Karen began.

"I know. Drew's resistant to having the mother around," Jean finished it out.

"I just wonder . . ." Karen joined in a kind of duet.

"Isn't it maddening? It's a sort of sick possessiveness."

"I've heard of stage mothers, devoting their whole lives to a movie child, but is Drew just being a surrogate mother?" Karen was glad to join in their assessment.

"You're not jealous, are you?" Jean asked.

"Heavens, how could I be jealous of a twelve or thirteen-year-old kid? It isn't anything you can put your finger on. It's just that Drew is absent-minded where I'm concerned. It's as though every working thought is about Aurora's exposure. I just wish Drew would pay more attention to me."

"Drew's concern is natural. That thirteen-year-old will be the making of the academy," Jean concluded.

By mid-December and during Christmas they were moving, taking Drew's van and twelve carloads of Jean's bedroom and kitchen materials down the four-mile stretch that ended in eastern Llangolen.

From the thirty miles to the east Anjelica brought in all her belongings from storage in Santa Maria. Her sewing machine was carried into the compound in the half-house where she would stay most of the day. They fixed the back of Jean's house, two smaller bedrooms, for the two of them while Jean moved her massive desk and her typewriter into the front sunporch with the windows facing the veranda. Her own bedroom was along the side. They hung the same bamboo curtains from before. Around the base of the veranda red geraniums sprawled in abundance, bathed in natural sea coast mists, freshly blooming in the gray mornings. In Jean's veranda room were stacks of books, her stereo system, and two desks—one desktop swept clean for a new project, the other ending in a flap for her typewriter.

By January they had their new quarters liveable. Jean stayed at home, quietly writing all day while Anjelica took Aurora away in the Volkswagon bug down to the compound. Anjelica stayed there in her sewing room and took Aurora her lunch on a tray where she was playing in the conservatory.

In this way they were able to take care of Aurora's six hour practice and still be close in a unit. Also, by moving, they had taken the child to a place safe from the gossip of the town, the sticking point having been where the child was housed in the compound as her living place. This way she could be with her mother, and the dragon lady wouldn't have anything to talk about.

They found themselves settling into a comfortable routine at night. Since Jean was at home all day, she would cook a main dish of lasagna or a fillet of beef Adrienne. Once a week a boeff bourguignon would be cut up if Jean expected Drew and Karen, as well as the others. Anjelica added a crusty French bread to the main dish which would be waiting on the stove, and Aurora was entrusted to toss the salad. At times, Jean was inspired to try a sophisticated dessert, a coupe Ambassadrice, perhaps, with raspberries, kirsch and peaches. Cold beef and ham from the previous day was all that was needed to complete the meal.

CHAPTER TWENTY-ONE

A Good Time of Life

Still close to Drew, but finding her time taken up by her writing, Jean found herself staying at home in the yellow house. They found the new arrangement to be homey. At night after the meal, they rested while Aurora picked out new music manuscript. It was a lovely time.

Three evenings a week when Drew dropped in for dinner, Jean would have a godmother's chicken mixed with white wine and tarragon, at the last minute a Madeira poured in, steaming with the lid on. After the salad course, Drew and Jean would lay the plans for the next publicity release or put together the program for the April concert.

Winter was approaching Llangolen. A heavy mist from the sea would seep in around the base of the house or a smoky rolling set of clouds poured in from the west, heralding a pelting cold rain like England and Wales. Together they clustered around the blackened wood stove in the square central room just off the veranda.

January passed. February too, and slowly their mulberry tree put forth buds, then a leaf. Slowly, too, some caring for each other began its insidious force. Drew seemed enchanted with the thirteen-and-a-half Aurora. To Karen's dismay and Jean's watchful eye, they saw what only could be termed a mutual admiration. Karen grew resentful at having to be at Jean's house nearly every day.

"Isn't it ridiculous?"

"What, Karen?"

"That a woman nearing forty should be..."

"So interested in that child."

"It's true she's sophisticated. And she's gifted. She's a real person already, interesting...and arresting..."

"Yeah, I know, but I feel as though I don't exist."

"It's just that Aurora is a big part of Drew's vision for the future."

"I caught her at home, writing poetry. It seemed to be directed toward Aurora!" Hateful eyes glared at Jean.

"You're imagining," Jean played for time.

"No, and I feel like hitting her."

"You can't hit a little girl. I know she can be exasperating and egocentric."

"Nobody else counts, and that goes for Drew, too," Karen finalized the statement as if it were an indictment.

As March came upon them, the feeling of interdependence and a bonding grew, not only between Drew and the budding genius, but Jean's feelings toward Anjelica Jacobson also took a new turn. Her deep sympathy for a mother trying to bring up a talented daughter increased, and Jean's need to have some sort of relationship, some settledness, so long repressed after the disaster of ten years before became satisfied. Anjelica could feel it too, a leaning in, since they were thrown closely together every day. She was released from too solid a team with her daughter.

One night Drew hurried in, hardly noticing the braised chicken and noodles steaming on her plate. She was obviously in a state of excitement. Only a tower of molded dessert appearing on the side table made her pause.

"What's this?"

"It's called Bavarian Cream Perfect Love."

They all spooned up the delicious confection with Drew barely concealing her good news.

"Oh, wow, I can't hold back with this any longer."

"We can see you're not going to stay speechless; it must be momentous."

"Yes, listen to this one. The phone rang with it just before I came up. I thought I would be late."

"From the agent?"

Anjelica was waiting, knowing it was about Aurora.

"Come on, Drew," her eyes were round.

"Yes, they want her. . .and guess where?"

"We can't." Jean put the perfectly-brewed coffee on the table.

"They want her at the Ambassador Auditorium. Ambassador! In Pasadena."

Aurora sucked in her breath and ran around the table. "What? I won't be ready. I need more practice."

"You have two months, really."

"Does it have to be original? Can I do Brahms?"

Drew gave her a hard look. "The program doesn't matter yet. The fact is, you've been chosen. It's for the best performing artists in Southern California."

"I won't go. I'm too scared. Not ready, mother...not..."

Anjelica looked at her daughter. "You can have the next month to decide the program. I'll see to it that you'll be ready. Your father would be ready. Agreed?"

Then Aurora looked at Drew. She couldn't let Drew down because that was the strength and beauty in this place.

"I know the Hayden. It might be ready. I've been lazing around on something else."

"I'll get you down there when the time comes," Drew said. "You and your mother. I know a relatively cheap place to stay right off the freeway. Anjelica can dress you. But Jean should stay here."

"Should she stay here all alone?" Anjelica questioned that decision.

"I'm needing to write," Jean said looking out at the yellow porch which was now home to her. The setting had been adapted to her specifications.

The house which had been ranch style with boxcar lines had been pushed out four feet to the jutting eves. They had moved a seventeen-foot-long section of the wall to the eave line to let them have room for a side foyer as they came in. This expanded their dining room where they lived at night. All this had been worked on in January, and by March it was completely painted and liveable.

The major change was to the rear. This adaptation gave room for a master bedroom in back. The rear addition extended back from the ridgeline and didn't distract from the street. From the road all that people could see in the front was veranda, a broad sweeping expanse of yellow and environmentally treated windows. Half of the veranda was screened for privacy. There was no door. All this front was Jean's spine, the interior expanse of writing room, cool enough in mornings, as well as sunny.

By March they had acquired a rootedness. Jean's attachment to Anjelica had increased. With Drew she felt a partnership. But Drew's strong cord to Aurora remained an enigma.

Jean conferred with Drew in late April. "We have to get some regulations ready for summer school. Who to let in, get the entrance requirements. We can invite some innovative people."

"Do you want everybody to be within eighteen and twenty-five?" Jean inquired.

"Yes, but we will make exceptions. You will have to provide housing for the students. And some of the teachers will have to get rooms in town and perhaps the smaller towns to the south. Be sure to tap the private beach homes who might like to make a little extra," Drew was helping now in the smaller management steps.

Already they had nine teachers at the school. Some had far-reaching reputations; some had settled at retirement in the little town, but were still giving lessons and lectures in music. One of the teachers enjoyed an international fame. Soon they would have to consider accreditation as a conservatory of music.

Aurora had been dropped into this milieu. They had waived her tuition fees. In other cases, they had reduced the price, and just now they were issuing information concerning students from abroad. In short, they were now a school that could give preparation for a professional performance career, a teaching position, or a post for a church.

Now, what a star to put in the brochure, to have someone asked to the Ambassador in Pasadena!

News of Aurora'a appointment spread fast, and musicians came to praise the new genius. Privacy was hard to preserve. Drew became more possessive of Aurora's time, and practice sessions were held inviolate, guests sometimes being able to listen from the low windows.

Early April storms kept people away from the compound. Harsh gales bit into the strands and seacliffs, but every day Aurora drove to her work, rattled in by Anjelica in the old Volkswagon. Each night they rested in the pleasant yellow frame house, usually after a peasant stew, French bread, fresh salad and Peaches Glaceé.

All day Jean kept at her desk, writing without interruption. Her typewriter stayed at the side portion of the large desk. She kept the other desk free to place new material. Pictures of her projected vision were pinned to the walls inside the windows. The latest addition she had placed there was a shot of the renovated and redecorated Carnegie Hall. Why not dream a little?

CHAPTER TWENTY-TWO

An Appointment in Pasadena

At this time in April, they got a week of real spring weather. The mornings were crisp, down to the 40's, rising to the 80's. "Jean, what are you doing up?" Anjelica looked in on her at six-thirty a.m.

"I'm always up at this time, just as the sun rises. I'm up here at my writing board."

"I thought you were absent when I go out with Aurora in the mornings."

"I'm right at my desk looking out the front garden. I write from six to ten every day."

"You mean, you put in four hours every morning?"

"Oh, more, but the other hour or two come after I put the manuscript away and start to braise the lamb shanks we're going to have with bulgar, pick the strawberries and make the cream puffs to put the cream in. You know, that good stuff we have every night."

"Well, I know it's been more fun, eating together, knowing where we belong at night," Anjelica looked out into a gentle movement of leaves rustling the pear tree. "If I have to move somewhere else, I'd miss what seems to be home. I'm gonna miss you, Jean."

Serene. The geraniums clustered around the lathes on the veranda outside. A Siamese cat observed the latest arrival which was a hummingbird dipping into white mock orange. This morning no motor noise came to them from the main road on the quiet end of town.

"I think I'll go along with you to Pasadena. Otherwise, I'd be alone with twenty people to organize for summer."

"There's safety in numbers..." murmured Anjelica, "maybe, I'll be thankful..."

"You mean, would I find distraction? In this rat race? There's too much to do. Anjelica, I'd miss you terribly if you went to L.A. for all those days without me," Jean leaned back in her typing chair. "I think I'll go."

Anjelica tried to be comfortable on the settee which was the only place not covered with papers. But there wasn't any way she could get closer to Jean who was sitting bolt upright at her typewriter. She wanted to put an arm around Jean, but it was awkward.

Everything came to a half. Jean was paralyzed in the chair. She felt a fine trace of fire under her skin, and in her right ear something drummed.

Just at that inopportune time, Aurora came to the partition doorjam and looked in impatiently.

"Mother!"

"I'll be getting along. Get everything ready."

"Drew's waiting for me!" Aurora snapped at her mother.

Jean felt a sharp urge to slap her out of her insensitivity to anything that was not her own musical genius. Damned brat! Other people had lives too. She rarely had time to get a full conversation with Anjelica without some interruption.

Aurora stood in the doorway scowling, looking like a statue of a young Greek girl and as hipless, like the young Spartan boys as "up to the age of twelve the little girl is as strong as her brother, and she shows the same mental powers," something Jean had noticed in an anthropological book by Charles Seltman, something called *Women in Antiquity.*

"Boy, same mental powers indeed," fumed Jean. "She was terribly obtuse when it came to anybody but her own music and possibly Drew. No consideration for anybody."

At this period in her life, Drew, the Directress, had become a woman of angular beauty. Her classic profile and figure was like Amelia Earhart in natural grace. Her hair had burnished strands of gold tied loosely in a quick knot at the base of her neck.

In contrast, Aurora was a budding girl-child. She had a narrow pelvic structure such as the models artists had been used to depicting in early Greek times with legs long and tapering into slender ankles. She had a mane of dark hair to the middle of her back.

The admiration Aurora felt for Drew was well deserved, for Drew was her teacher, both in notes and harmony, and Drew was the driving force behind this new school for women musicians. Drew was well-trained with an intelligence that could command a project of great dimension. Her force of personality magnetized friends who donated the money for the school. In short, it wouldn't have been drawn together without Drew.

And why not Aurora? Why shouldn't she be attracted thought Jean? She felt a bit jealous of their closeness. The cohesiveness puzzled and irritated her. Why should Drew turn her affection toward someone so young? It seemed to Jean that several times she had seen them disappear under the pines as if with some great secret. Also, Drew had a way of letting the top of her garment down carelessly, as if to show the fine line of her bosom. Jean had no claim on Drew, but it was almost as if the student-teacher attraction was exaggerated. They were both amorous and inseparable.

As the time approached for the trip to Pasadena, Jean saw Drew and Aurora with their heads together. Along the side of the conservatory, Jean was walking one day and came upon Drew looking at Aurora's hand. She seemed to be measuring a finger.

Troubled, she turned to Anjelica for some kind of explanation.

"Don't worry so much. You know that as young girls grow up they have a kind of hero worship for their teachers. That doesn't necessarily mean anything is wrong."

"But it's hiding Drew away from me," wailed Jean.

"Not really. Besides, you have me to worry about." In her feminine way, Anjelica softened the hurt. "You really are worthy, you know. Don't you know how you count with me?"

Anjelica semi-leaned toward Jean before Aurora's impatient call from the open door of the Volkswagon pulled her away from the veranda and Jean.

CHAPTER TWENTY-THREE

Lived Time, Well Timed

The home for the performing arts, the Ambassador, decided the booking and the program. They welcomed the finest young artists in the world. Located in Pasadena, California, the Ambassador offered a varied selection of series, opera stars, pianists, and superb soloists of all periods. To be selected was a big triumph for Aurora. The news stories gave her credit, and the compound was hectic during the days of early May as they made final preparations.

As if to complicate matters, Drew received urgent phone calls from New York, indicating that there might be a chance for Aurora to play in Carnegie Hall. First, however, they had to take care of the immediate problem which was to transport Aurora to Southern California. The freeway heading east from Highway 101 took only minutes. This was their accessible route. Drew and Jean and Aurora confirmed the booking which was early May, and they decided to stick to this booking because it wouldn't necessarily throw them off from a plan Drew had had to try for the Carnegie.

As they got to a Pasadena hotel to occupy their rooms, Jean spoke to Anjelica. "This is getting a reward, Anjelica, look at all the pressure you had to apply to make her practice."

"Yeah, some credit, but think of the sulky looks, really horrid at times."

Aurora ignored the chitchat in the back seat, immersed in the nearness of Drew. She was honored to be in her presence. She lingered near her for as long as she could, trying to prolong the inspiring essence. To her, this famous person had lived so many years beyond her, and so many friends had claim on Drew's time that she felt honored to be near the goddess, like an early priestess. Aurora had adoration for a mystical being whose life span had preceded hers.

They all piled into the foyer of the hotel just as Anjelica was stating, "And her first big chance at thirteen and New York by fourteen, we hope."

For Drew the feelings she had the night of the 20th were hard to explain. The magic of the girl on the stage would remain throughout a lifetime. At eight o'clock Aurora came out, long mane of hair down to her elbows, her slight body in a gown with a sunburst on the front stylized with orange and black accent. She appeared to be, not a lion, but a Japanese Noh player. This night was to be a lived moment. Drew was aware with all the nerves of her body, listening, looking.

Aurora walked to a superb baby grand piano one minute after eight, and as the audience hushed, lowered her head, hair, and driving hands over the keyboard, slowly then lower, lower, head down over a trilling ripple of the Brahms. Resonant bass notes made an extra voice pulling against high notes.

All the time and attention of her mother were paying off. Aurora was impressive, young and powerful.

Sometimes her head and hair were drooping over the keys: sometimes there was movement over the keyboard. Climbing, busy notes. Aurora was working now diligently at her task and showed her love for her piano.

Drew felt hard-pressed to give expression to what the music meant, but it revealed the tension of mind that we feel in our lives.

Aurora strained to the keyboard as if she were faced with an animal fleeing in the wood and she was trying to charm it back into captivity. At times she raised her eyebrows, pleading with her opposite animus. On the whole, the unity of the concert was unbroken. The request number from the audience was one of the movements she had done from Brahms, not so stunning as the time spent playing the other pieces.

Trills of upward notes, counterpoint, a flight. The bass chords tripped over each other, flying over valleys and swales. Here Aurora was bending and swaying over some task constantly beyond her reach. She played right through this, sometimes the hard force of her fingers making her cheeks shake. The upper arm muscles showed definition changed by the pressure of her hands, then there was a rocking motion. The left arm came up into view.

Most of the time Aurora showed pleasure, being a friend with her piano, playing games. Under the spotlight she made a team with her white-keyed partner.

Aurora had placed a glittering headband in her black mane; under it her face was quizzical. Then suddenly tired at the end, her face looked Japanese, Greek—anyway, pretty. It was a sweet face.

The audience was well-behaved, mature, gray polls among them, respectful and ready to hear. The invited artists brought in a multi-languaged audience, many of them from the wealthy part of Pasadena.

Now returning after intermission, Aurora came on stage in a black bodice. Now the Schubert.

For a long period, she sat with arms gripping both elbows. Then she bent toward the keys, lower and lower her head, right to the keys, exactly.

All was motionless in the hall. Expressively, tenderly, Aurora played a love song to the Schubert—a repetitive melody. Her girdled orange on black toga bent back once, then her arms made many small notes sound as one sound. She was tired now, her task was finished.

She made no response to the clamoring crowd. There was still a group to meet down in the basement, off the stage, past the two-inch pile of blue-purple carpet.

"Shall we let her see them?"

"Wait, we'll have to," said Anjelica, knowing her daughter's right to grasp the reward, even though she was exhausted. Beyond the purple was a deep yellow carpet with red plush ottomans. A door opened and closed. She was not yet recovered.

Outside the theater doors, chandeliers still sparkled and the audience milled, satisfied, not leaving rapidly but leisurely. Most lived nearby. Orange lights on the outside reflected in the watered pool surrounding the theater.

At last, Aurora came to the door to admit the admirers gathered to honor her. Her efforts had drenched her, dampened her hair. Her face turned immediately to Drew as Anjelica winced at being unacknowledged.

Finally, the hall emptied as the last attendants left in their cars. They all piled tiredly into Drew's van. Jean drove them this time right down to the exit ramp which took them to Highway 134 across the San Fernando Basin and from there a midnight ride through Santa Maria and then home to Llangolen at three in the morning.

At seven-thirty, after four hours of restless sleep, Jean and Drew were awakened by a jingling telephone.

There was a squawking voice, "Have you seen the papers?"

"No paper. Haven't got up yet."

Drew replaced the receiver. The phone kept ringing. It rang all morning long.

This engagement established them in the music community. A new genius was announced in the L.A. papers, and people in Llangolen were ecstatic.

Four local artists of varied instrumental fame offered a stimulating program the following weekend in Llangolen featuring their new star, Aurora, together with Drew, the Directress of the School.

Everyone was bubbling with enthusiasm in the old formal hall. They had just quieted down to hear a flutist do a piece from Mozart, when behind in the foyer some commotion disturbed the melodic leaps.

There in the doorway, racketing about with her crutches, was the once formidable Mrs. McGrag. She had deteriorated since Drew last saw her. Now her figure was voluminous; she billowed. Something was wrong with her leg, hence, she used the crutches. She staggered and clanged about for a full three minutes while the flutist waited. Then she collapsed like a spent balloon, her baggy cheeks shaking.

Her face was blotchy, sagging at the neck. When she smiled in a ghastly way, one yellowed tooth protruded. Most noticeable was a patch over the eye. It appeared that she had only one eye. Here, indeed, was the monster foretold by Drew's aunt. "She would destroy a monster."

Mrs. McGrag fell into her seat with a gasp. Then the flutist was allowed to continue. But at intermission, she mingled with the other guests, her grayish cheeks shaking as she glared balefully at the chief source of celebration, Aurora. Mrs. McGrag's eye was red-rimmed and filled with passionate hate. She could not destroy them now. The girl pianist had obviously attained her triumph.

The guests whispered among themselves about the alcoholic coming out for public appearance. The disturbance in the music hall was noticed by everyone, but if Mrs. McGrag only wanted to harass and worry them with her frequent attacks, she wasn't successful. The final piece was played to the quiet of the hall, and at the end there was tumultuous applause. Mrs. McGrag dispersed in the crowd, and this was her final debut as chief dragon of the community.

However, Drew's vindictive stare softened as she looked at the woman's face from a distance. Those harsh lines on either side of Mrs. McGrag's nose; there was something about this that reminded Drew of her own mother. Indeed, could it possibly be that Drew might herself come to resemble one of these women? Hitherto she had been scornful, even cruel to the bothersome McGrag. She may have, in a way destroyed what might have been her own mother. It may have been that Drew contributed to the symbolic demise of this woman.

Drew thoughtfully pulled Jean aside and whispered, "Maybe she just wanted to be included in the action at the school. We should have drawn her in."

Jean's eyes met hers in understanding, ". . . asked her to help us. We all, after all, are part of a continuity. I'm a little sorry too."

CHAPTER TWENTY-FOUR

Drew's Captive Goes East

During the last weeks in April, Drew had made constant efforts with telegram and telephone to complete an engagement at the Carnegie Hall. It materialized in a booking to replace a last-minute cancellation of a soprano. Could Aurora be readied to fit in toward the end of their season?

Such short notice made them hurry, but since Aurora had just finished in Pasadena, maybe she could use part of the same program, such as the Bach English Suite No. 2 in A-Minor and then a Shubert sonata.

Late one night over chicken stewed in sherry the Mexican way, they conferred over the trip East which they had agreed to. Aurora was going to have her debut at the Recital Hall in the Carnegie, a place coveted by the younger musicians. The date was to be May 25, the closing of the concert season.

As they talked it over, Jean determined that she was needed more in the compound at Llangolen. Gretyl, it seemed, had better go instead of Jean, so as to provide practical support and food for the four of them.

Anjelica was familiar with New York, having lived there, but in a tenement section. She was puzzled about where they would be staying.

"What hotel could we find that would be close?"

"It's pretty certain that we will stay at the Salisbury across the street from Carnegie Hall." Drew had already made plans.

"Oh, that close?" Anjelica was pleased.

"We can all be there together. We can stay in a suite where four people can have more room, even a kitchenette, so we won't have to go out every night," Drew continued.

Anjelica concurred in having Gretyl go along. "She can feed us so much cheaper, and I can look over Aurora's clothes. That would cut down expense."

"It's the same as a double in one of the other hotels. It's better not to be rushing around with thousands of people in downtown

New York anyway. Drew had made up her mind.

"I know we can't stay out in Brooklyn," Anjelica was contented to let Drew confirm the hotel.

The time came sooner than they thought, and as they left on the plane, they all said goodbye to Jean who had driven them to the airport. They were so excited that they didn't notice Jean's fond embrace of Anjelica who was telling her they would hurry back and that she was going to be missed.

They landed in New York without mishap and were hurried in the taxi to West 57th Street.

People were whizzing by on foot and in cabs. They made tracks, too, getting all their luggage into a suite at the moderately-priced hotel. Across the street was the Carnegie, looking like modified Renaissance eclectic, almost a Romanesque look to the facade.

They pushed their way into the foyer of the marbled hall moving back to the auditorium with its rich red plush and gilt paint. In the central hall there were two tiers of box seating with the special one for Andrew Carnegie in the first tier. They counted sixty-three boxes.

But the busier room was the Recital Hall in the adjoining room. Here was the most coveted place where Aurora would play. The Juliard and Manhattan School of Music artists loved to pay to have their debuts in the room that would seat 300. The larger hall was generally the place for string quartets.

Aurora ran through an adjoining door to the Rose Room below which was connected so that admirers could come to pay their respects. This was to be her place to triumph or be ignored in the string of recitals that crowded a busy season. In two days she would know the tale.

The bigger main hall had been the scene of Van Cliburn who had made his debut at the age of twelve with the Houston Symphony. In 1954 he had won the Edgar N. Levintritt Award, entitling him to a Carnegie Hall Concert which took place on a Sunday afternoon with Dimitri Mitropoulos playing Tchaikovsky's B-Flat Minor Concerto. Cliburn received seven curtain calls at that time.

Aurora was going to be in the recital hall. No one else was in there with her on the program. She looked briefly at the beautiful grand piano which, together with the stool, were the only objects beneath the heavily-swagged upper curtain. She seated herself at the stool to get positioned, in awe of the people who had been there before her. She sat there a moment, then Anjelica and Drew escorted her into the comfortable room at the Salisbury.

Drew helped Aurora to unpack, placing her in the other twin in her room. In an adjoining room, Anjelica and Gretyl found their beds, and in an adjoining room a dining table gave them a central place to eat and keep records. Drew insisted that Aurora go to bed immediately, closed the accordion door on her, and the other three gathered together to set their plans for the day before the concert. Aurora would have to practice soon, but around three in the afternoon Drew wanted to take her off to shop in busy Fifth Avenue. Anjelica grew more puzzled at the way Drew seemed to be taking over her daughter, and she tried to resist this latest plan, but Drew was insistent.

"Okay, have it your way. We'll just take a boat around Manhattan while you're doing that." Anjelica gave in, seeing that Drew didn't want her with them.

"No, go see if you can find out anything more about the hall itself," urged Drew. "We should know the history of things that have happened here. Gretyl, you go research some stuff and share it with us later on in the day."

"Yes, we'll have to be prepared to tell reporters in the West when we return home," Gretyl said. "I have to be in charge of what to tell the papers."

Instead of sightseeing with Anjelica next morning, Gretyl set out for the Public Library with its magnificent stone lions. There she learned how musicians of all kinds praised the sound of the Great Hall's accoustical effects. The architect William Tuthill used rounded architectural details in the auditorium, and the fact that the walls were four feet thick helped. There was a resonating space under the stage that helped the sound. Even the seats were covered with a thick fabric to add to the enjoyment of the audience.

To get to the cheaper seats, viewers have to climb and struggle 135 steps. Here, viewers in 1927, were able to hear the young

Yehudi Menuhin, who when he explored around backstage and encountered a fireman's axe, asked what it was for, was met with a solemn reply, "to chop the heads off soloists who don't play well." "And how many heads has it chopped?" "Quite a few," said the guard, and the fat little boy scampered back to the room to practice." This story had been told to *Life* reporters.

Here it was that the Horowitz nails came into being, two of them pounded into the stage floor as stagehands tired of moving a huge grand piano around. The downstage nails of Horowitz's piano had been placed on a special spot for favored accoustical perfection.

The following night, Gretyl told them what she had learned. The Carnegie was also the setting for Judy Garland's triumph, only to be followed by Liza Minelli's eleven-in-a-row sold-out shows. Liza displayed pictures of her mother on the dressing room walls, and on her final night stood at the empty stage and sobbed.

Gretyl finally concluded with the story of the debuts which came at the Recital Hall rather than the Hall itself, such as that of Van Cliburn who made his debut on that very stage and at the same age as Aurora.

Aurora opened the *New York Times*. They had reported her to be a protegé Andre Previn as Drew, herself, was mentioned as the Directress of the new Llangolen School for Music. As they finally settled down for sleep that night, a call came in from the West as Jean wanted to know how things were going, but Anjelica put her off with a quick call, wanting to talk to her alone.

"I'll call you back in two hours, exactly. These people are dead on their feet."

For two hours at the table by the telephone, Anjelica sat in confusion while the rest were sleeping. She missed Jean. Wandering around the room she shared with Gretyl, she wondered when it would be safe to call back. Privacy was hard to come by. Finally, she decided to wait until morning, knowing that everyone would be gone by eight.

The next day, Drew and Aurora dressed and left, and Anjelica dialed the number of their Llangolen home, knowing Jean was up already at her writing.

"I'm so unsure of what I want, but I just had to call," Anjelica faltered.

"I know, I don't know how you feel. I'm just waiting for you to come home. We haven't had any time together."

"How are we going to fix that? It will be five days from now, and I'll be so tired when you pick us all up. Then, too, how are we going to get away since we'll all be at the house?" Anjelica worried aloud.

"Let's make a date. Is it a date?" Jean's voice was unsure.

"By Wednesday we should all be rested up. I'll make an excuse that we're needed over in San Luis, and we'll simply leave together. It's a date, then."

They talked together for the rest of the hour. Then Anjelica rang off to fix a light meal for the rest when they returned from their second trip along the city streets. Finally, Gretyl returned with a second bulging briefcase full of the Carnegie information from the library.

Excitedly, she told them more of Paderewski and Minelli memories as they munched on bagels and cream cheese, nut bread, and blintzes. They had their own triumphant world perched high in the dusky city.

As they yawned and slid into their beds, Anjelica sneaked over to the connecting room and again called Jean. She was awake and waiting.

"How's it going?"

"Shhh...I have to whisper. It's lonely here without you. I haven't even left the suite. I'm so wishing these five days will evaporate. I want to be with you. Drew's gone out and bought something, jewelry for Aurora, I think it's a ring."

"Maybe you need one, too," faltered Jean. "Come home here, and I'll get you one. How will I get along with you?"

"Remember our date. We'll get away on Wednesday, I promise. They're exhausted enough already and tomorrow is the performance."

"Don't worry about presents," returned Jean. "Just get home here where your real life is beginning with me."

The next day, the recital day, Gretyl kept Aurora busy. There was no practice for her on this day of days. The telephone rang constantly, but Gretyl expertly gave a story to each journalist. She loved the restless excitement. Anjelica was hoping Friday night would be over.

When it finally arrived, all three of them looked out their windows across at the evening concert-goers gathering at the front of the brown and buff-contrasted hall. Inside the suite, Aurora rested.

Anjelica had dressed the girl to perfection. One last minute strap in her shoe had to be fixed with a rubber band.

At last, the coveted invitation came to fruition as they all walked solemnly out the side door, down one alley and onto a street, entering the hall from the side. They placed Aurora in the Rose Room with the stage manager and Anjelica. Drew and Gretyl left the nervous mother and re-entered the hall to get two of the center seats in the first tier.

For Drew, the recital had a major incantation. There was more maturity in Aurora's mannerisms. Her hair was luxuriant. She had the same sunburst-on-black gown, only her figure was growing nubile. And her attack for sound in this piano was beautiful in itself. She had no trouble with the Ravel "Tzigane." She worked off Shubert's E-flat Piano Sonata as if it meant something to her, had got under her skin. She was competent and professional as she finished off the finale.

The audience rose to their feet. All 300 people rose and gave thirteen curtain calls, to their astonishment. She was an acclaimed new arrival in the rank of a major performing artist. The young girl had stretched to the prize.

Drew was feeling that she had hatched out a goddess-priestess. There was something mysterious and non-human about Aurora. Drew felt that they would grow together for a long period. The girl was needed by the school as virtuoso, and Drew could shelter her there.

Many flowers were pressed on Aurora when she entered the Rose Room. They raved over her technical proficiency and were amazed by her dawning beauty. The young were pressed around her in droves, however, evening dress prevailed. After an hour, Aurora pronounced herself tired.

They found their way out the side door and into their suite at the Salisbury. On the center table was a carton of fruit and flowers from Jean. They brought up a light supper of sandwiches and a sweet golden wine, but Aurora was off to bed. They closed off the curtains and had a triumph feast for the three of them, waiting for the papers, but intending to get a few hours of rest.

At seven, Drew woke up Aurora with a stack of reviews. "There's nothing to hurt," she said quickly, stroking her long hair. "No deficiencies, interesting technical command, pulling the notes from a loved animal," the *Times* had said.

"Do you think?" began Aurora.

"You've arrived in the musical world. They know who. . ."

"Who I am? Am I a hit?"

"Don't you know and feel it? Not one memory slip, no blunting of tone cluster. They just loved you."

"Well," started out Aurora, but she was beginning to be convinced. "I know I'm young, but I still feel there is a lot left in me. What a terribly happy time! I've got my mother caring for me, we're settled, and I've got you, Drew."

"And New York, too!"

"Let's go home, Drew, perfect happiness. I want to go to work by the sea. I can't wait to see their faces and the lush green of our compound. And the blue haze off the sea!"

Anjelica added, "What I want to see is the yellow veranda."

Drew picked up the phone. "Let's see if there is anyone there at the yellow veranda. Someone you know."

They put through a triumphant call. The school would be all the better for this stellar performance, reflected Drew.

They re-entered Los Angeles late at night and Jean was at the airport to meet them. She drove all night on Highway 101, and by nine o'clock in the early morning, they were coming up through Llangolen. A parade was coming up the street to greet them, a victory parade. The local school had readied a performance.

They put Aurora in a convertible, also Drew. And most of the membership of the compound was there with the townspeople to greet their first celebrity. This was the first time they had showed approval. When they approached the brick road to the compound, four of the local artists were at the top to greet them.

Suddenly, Drew became conscious of how shocking her relationship with Aurora might seem. The future seemed rocky, maybe an unhappy ending lay ahead. Her love for Aurora was reciprocated, but on another plane. "I can't imagine how she feels for me, but outside of the sexual feelings, I only want to protect her as a young talent." She glanced at Aurora.

Sitting beside Drew, Aurora also was having an uncomfortable time as the crowd stared. Inwardly she thought, "I do love her and would like to enhance her life, with mine of music. Also, I want her to stick to things especially here at the school. She seemed to drop people so fast, especially in that druggy time."

Finally, the two glanced at each other, proud and yet anxious under the stares of the others. Aurora thought briefly of their physical contact and retreated. The quality of their emotional state was not equal.

And Drew, glancing at her troubled look, stirred inside herself in her wish to see into Aurora's mind.

She was anxious about Aurora's leaving home for two years. What would happen to the two of them? Aurora would become another person. Still, it would be a good idea to give her all that training. The Viennese invitation was solid, happening after Christmas and into the new year. In the meantime, they needed a West Coast exposure.

Over the dining room table, the four heads were bent, two blonde and two black, looking at a spread-out nap of Austria, Switzerland, and Germany.

"We're just looking, you understand," Drew was saying. "We're not that ready to send you away. You're evidently needed here, you know."

"Well, I need my time here to practice. It's serene; we're..." Aurora broke off.

"Settled. You might say. Very settled for now," Drew was on a continuous high after the Carnegie Hall triumph.

"I know and I don't want to leave you. And mother, too," she added. "...and Jean."

"You know," Jean said, "just when we're getting known here and have things to our liking, we ought not to haul up and go away, leaving the school. You're our prize pupil."

"Yeah, we need you here," Drew puzzled her forehead. "I'm getting busier all the time," and then she stopped, wondering...

"About all that old story my aunt had been telling my family long ago..."

"You mean about your unconventional marriage?" smiled Jean.

"Well, no about the rock. There was something more to it, about a rock being the making of me or my..."

"Early demise?"

"Yeah, die. I could throw myself from the rock like Sappho."

"Rock, what rock? What about the rock?"

"There is a rock as we well know, and it's in the town down from here. You know, it ends that eight peak volcanic formation that winds like an S through San Luis Obispo County. What...could it mean?" Jean puzzled over it.

"Well, really," insisted Drew. "Let me follow my thought." In a bemused way, she muttered low, "The rock could lend itself to a major setting for a lot of people coming in from L.A., all over. It's a key landmark and people from distant parts know about it. It stands way up over 500 feet from the ocean."

"Yes, but that's a long shot, so what about it?"

"I know," went on Drew. "I'm confused, but it seems to me that rock is a high point in my life."

"Of course, and right now your life is tied up with Aurora's." Jean emphasized as she looked over at the sleeping Aurora. Her face wrinkled with worry as she reflected on what was going on between the two. There would be problems in a few years.

"Listen, as long as we're planning the school for the summer, why couldn't we propose a five-year future?"

"What would be the first element?"

"I'm starting to think we need to have a...concert by the sea, something like Monterey," Drew added. "Only with the rock as a focal point."

"Yah!" Jean and Anjelica looked at each other as though they had thought it up themselves.

Aurora looked up sleepily.

"What was that?" she had been half listening.

"Oh, something about having you play out on a rock."

"We could get it out there, you know," Drew looked over at Jean. "You could make the rock a place to head for. People would stay at all the local places, even the state park."

"Could that possibly be a part of the prophesy? The meaning of the rock?" Jean looked at her. "I thought you were going to lose your *life* on a rock."

"Rock already tried that and failed," Drew insisted.

"Still," and a nagging thought drifted at the top of her head. She might lose her active life, her full powers as a result of this place where Aurora was going to play.

* * *

Drew made several trips into Santa Barbara to connect with the existing network of publicity. She was a drawing card because she had entrée to several societies in the wealthy area. She knew many notable people in the music world and they had parties which made preview announcement of the forthcoming concert. Soon the advance tickets were set up in Ticketron, and various publications paid for advertisements.

Jean was busy writing news releases. Because of the connections, they made advance sales for the October 1 concert. By August and September they felt the slack-off from summer school session and were confident they would meet the opening date. Most of the motels stretching across the five city beach towns were booked up in blocks, with Jean and Gretyl handling room reservations.

Aurora practiced six hours daily to be ready for the performance. She climbed the rock and looked at the various aspects of Estero Bay. Hans and some men had planned to move the piano on the day of the concert to prevent injury to its fine wood. The coastal authorities had to give clearance, along with the harbor master, but they received their approval.

As the weekend approached, visitors began filling in the rooms and swelling the restaurants and streets of the picturesque fishing village of Morro Bay. The cluster of harbor cafes, bobbing yachts, and local fishing men gave an authentic air of genuineness, a direct contrast to an L.A. traffic-filled street. The slow moving tourists sauntered past sea shell stores and aquariums, stopped to sample fresh shrimp cocktails at the Finicky Fish II, and stopped to watch actual fishing catches being unloaded from the trawlers. Down the main parkways the special eucalyptus trees, *Ficus folius,* flowered with their dusty pinks and corals. The tourists forgot their hurry and impatience and simply enjoyed the seacoast ambiance. There is nothing fake about Morro Bay.

Meanwhile, ten miles to the north, Aurora practiced in the concert room. She seemed to become more beautiful. Her hands were slender with long fingers, and Drew would linger over their shapeliness.

"Your hands! There are no others, not one in a hundred thousand!"

They sat together under the pines of Llangolen. Aurora would respond, "I love the ring you bought for me."

At these times, Anjelica scarcely knew she had a daughter because of the long practice hours in the dusty Indian summer. She, herself, kept busy at the news material demanded by the reporters. And she worried about the strangeness of the relationship.

* * *

The morning of the concert broke to a clear sky. Down at the marina, many sailboats were beginning to cast off, angling like swans among some rusty brown ducks clustering the harbor. The craft had no trouble anchoring in the channel because this day the water was calm and sheltered from the sea. A low tide had promised little difficulty and there were scarcely any waves.

Soon the quay was covered with people and cars. Out on the long largo sand spit where drifting material had to be lifted out of the channel, the drifts were covered with picknickers. By four o'clock, it was black with concert-goers who had walked miles from where the beginnings of the sand began, down to where the key broke off for the boat channel.

Together in the yellow veranda, the four quietly made the last preparations. By now, their common purpose had pulled them together into harmony. Aurora was ready to perform. They shared a light lunch of clam chowder and artichokes, crusty French bread, and by six they were piled into Drew's van.

The piano had been lovingly hoisted to the rock by ten in the morning. All the four had to do was to get Aurora there in time for the event which was seven-thirty, the first day in October. As they rounded the steep bend leading to the harbor road, they had to be led in by a pair of motorcycle police.

Thousands of people clustered below the rock, in cars and on foot, blankets spread out. In the pearly blue harbor, in the narrow straights and beyond, hundreds of boats held their places, and Tiger's Folly had steamed in by paddle wheel directly in the center of the bay.

Along the edges of the sea, out past the breakwater, the far surf was tinged with lavender, and for some reason the waves lapping alongside the boats had a rose-blue tint. Drew and Jean left the van in the shade of the rock which was outlined by the setting sun, and the four together began their ascent to the base of the rock.

Now, Aurora and Drew together climbed up to the rocky outcropping where the piano stood. Finally Drew rose, tall and stately in a pleated tunic robe to announce the beginning. The crowd was hushed as Aurora struck up the first bars of the Brahms concerto.

For one hour and a quarter, she poured out a heartbreaking stream of notes, a melange of familiar and sometimes strange chords. All too soon, the triumph was over, and they were transported down the road in a happy confusion.

In her mind, Drew reverted to an earlier scene, that of a stormswept sea. There in her direct extremity, wave-bashed and rockbashed, she had witnessed the Pacific in another mood.

She remembered how sandy waves had battered her and her smaller friend, how the harbor had looked so wintry as they staggered in bloody disarray toward the coast guard building. Then, the eucalyptus strands had whipped straight out in the wind. Their sailboat canvas had billowed and stiffened under the storm. Now she had beaten it, conquered the wind, even conquered the rock.

In addition, the helpless feeling of being caught into somebody else's power trip was gone. Drew was in control of her own school; she was not a small schoolteacher in a bureaucratic windstorm. She was happy, too, for being able to win herself a decent independence. Still, there were flaws. She would age, when twenty years were piled on her, she would be a woman of 63. Then . . . she might get treated the way they had treated the miserable McGrag who had destroyed herself by her own vindictiveness. But as for now, well, she was in it, wasn't she?

* * *

By that month's end, Drew and Aurora were off to Vienna for the winter concerts, but Anjelica remained behind with Jean. The hunger for a permanent love, the longing for a person who cared, and to be with someone she loved, this had been given to Jean. She was pegged to a house by the sea, at least to the edge of Llangolen, and she had, at last, a sense of permanence. She was happy.

Let Drew and Aurora be the vagabonds. They could wander outside. They were set to take lodging for a time, for four or five months, in the old Russian Embassy ten miles from Vienna. Let them go, thought Jean, they would return to Llangolen by the sea, in June or July. She would be around to greet them on her own yellow verandah!